Triggadale

Elijah R. Freeman

**Lock Down Publications and
Ca$h Presents**
Triggadale
A Novel by Elijah R. Freeman

Triggadale
Lock Down Publications
P.O. Box 870494
Mesquite, Tx 75187

Visit our website
www.lockdownpublications.com

Lock Down Publications
Like our page on Facebook: Lock Down Publications @
www.facebook.com/lockdownpublications.ldp
Cover design and layout by: **Dynasty Cover Me**
Book interior design by: **Shawn Walker**
Edited by: **Lauren Burton**

Elijah R. Freeman
Stay Connected with Us!

Text **LOCKDOWN** to 22828 to stay up-to-date with new releases, sneak peeks, contests and more…

Triggadale
Submission Guideline.

Submit the first three chapters of your completed manuscript to ldpsubmissions@gmail.com, subject line: Your book's title. The manuscript must be in a .doc file and sent as an attachment. The document should be in Times New Roman, double-spaced and in size 12 font. Also, provide your synopsis and full contact information. If sending multiple submissions, they must each be in a separate email.

Have a story but no way to send it electronically? You can still submit to LDP/Ca$h Presents. Send in the first three chapters, written or typed, of your completed manuscript to:

LDP: Submissions Dept
Po Box 870494
Mesquite, Tx 75187

DO NOT send original manuscript. Must be a duplicate.

Provide your synopsis and a cover letter containing your full contact information.

Thanks for considering LDP and Ca$h Presents.

Elijah R. Freeman

Prologue

Click-clack!

The sound was barely detectable, yet ominous. "Oh, shit! What the –"

Omar's words were cut short as the butt of the gun slammed forcefully against the side of his head, sending him crumbling to ground. As his face smacked the pavement, his keys fell from his hand. "Argh, fuck!" he groaned, holding his head just above his right eyebrow in a futile attempt to stop the flow of warm blood that leaked from the huge gash.

"Run that shit!" a deep voice commanded.

Omar's head was spinning, but he managed to look up through the fog in his head and the blood that ran down into his eye. What stared back down at him were two dread-heads, and both of them held .9 millimeters that were aimed at his head.

Within seconds their identities registered in Omar's mind. Huncho and Flame. The night skyline made them look even more sinister than the weapons. Omar looked back and forth between the two men, finally settling his gaze on one. He held up a hand in semi-surrender. "Goddamn, Flame, what's up?"

The question was reactionary because the answer was obvious. He had pulled up off of Valley Hill to meet Flame on a back street to cop three ounces of popcorn mid. Now it was some fuckery in the game.

"Bitch, you heard what my nigga said. Run that shit or get clapped!" barked Huncho with his finger on the trigga, ready to make the nine spark.

Omar balled up his face in disbelief. "Man, you really gon' do me like this?"

Pow! Flame let off a warning shot inches from Omar's head. "Nigga, this ain't no game. Play wit' it if you want to, bet you be at Heaven's door!"

That sizzling hot bullet close to Omar's dome convinced him that testing these niggas would turn a robbery into a homicide. "A'ight, brah, you got that," he wisely surrendered.

Reluctantly, Omar gave up his money and his chains. Flame grabbed Omar's car keys while Huncho made him lay out flat on his stomach with his arms stretched out. He patted Omar down thoroughly, making sure he wasn't strapped. When he was done, he threatened, "If you get up before we bend the corner, I'ma pop ya stupid ass!"

Huncho hurried off and hopped in his Dodge Charger just as his partner-in-crime was pulling away in Omar's Nissan Altima. Another successful caper without any clap-back. The two friends felt invincible as they lashed out.

Jackboys by trade, armed robbery was their go-to grind. They were only teenagers, and already they'd robbed so many. Their favorite marks were grown men like the two they'd left naked and stranded. It made them feel some type of way.

Two blocks later Flame tossed the keys in a sewer, and before long they were at a trap house off Old Roundtree Road. As soon as they crossed the threshold, the jewelry was sold. Pockets straight from the lick, they climbed in Huncho's smoke-gray Dodge Charger and hit Southlake Mall to cop a couple fits from Street Stuff, an urban clothing store.

Huncho admired his new gear in the dressing room mirror: black Air Max 95s, black Girbaud jeans with the white straps, and a tall black tee. Under the light his dark skin gleamed, and on his right wrist was a black Nike wristband. His clothes were baggy like most kids his age, and they hung from his tall, lanky frame. Blonde-tipped dreads draped his shoulders, and on his head he wore an all-black 'A' fitted backward. He bent down to brush some lint off his J's and his dreads hung, surrounding his face. Spotting a scuff, he licked his thumb and rubbed at it until it vanished. He stood upright and flashed his mug to check out the gleam of gold in his bottom row of teeth.

Satisfied, he grabbed his bags and stepped out of the dressing room and into the store. Huncho approached the register to find Flame already there, getting his fits rung up by the thick, Hispanic cashier with long red hair. Huncho licked his lips at the sight.

Flame did a double-take back at Huncho and threw his arms up wide. His lips were quirked to the side in confidence. "So, I ain't fresh as hell?"

Huncho couldn't help but smile. Not only was his right-hand fresh to death, he was feelin' himself. No one could tell Flame shit right then. He stood mid-height with brown skin and thick, blonde-tip dreads that hung only inches above his waist and lower back. Gray, black, and white covered him from his low-top Forces, to his San Antonio Spurs jersey, under which he wore no t-shirt. Gray Dickies sagged around his thighs, and his bare arms were exposed, showing off his athletic build.

"Sho is," Huncho embraced Flame in a handshake hug. "Almost as fresh as me."

Three hours later they were pulling up to the Brooke's Crossing Apartments off Taylor Road. They were feeling themselves and wanted to show face with the twin sisters they pulled last week at a kickback in Park Ridge – Diamond and Destiny. Both were slender and had a healthy, yellow skin tone and nice, perky breasts. The only telltale sign between them was their hair. Destiny's was long while Diamond wore hers in a short do.

They got their shine on, flashing money and firing up back-to-back blunts. Sex was tempting, but they didn't feel like showering before they hit Sparkles, and hit Sparkles they would. It was Saturday, which was teen night, the night when the rink became a dance floor for teenagers. This was their hangout. They were there every Saturday faithfully. In fact, so was every teen in Riverdale who was anybody. Surrounding counties, too. It was one of the hottest chill spots on the Southside for teens. Paying security extra to gain access to 'eighteen and older' clubs was also common practice, but Saturday nights at Sparkles had become somewhat of a ritual. It was where everyone came to show off and where cliques came to get their music spent.

Huncho and Flame were both well-respected members of Southside Mafia, a local street gang that was growing and increasing its size daily. It was said they were over a hundred deep in number. They were identified by their blonde-tip dreads and the upside down 'W' they threw up to form an 'M' for 'Mafia' whenever they felt the need to rep their set and side of town.

They paid ten dollars at the door and walked in with Silencer, MJ, and Big B, a few Mafiosos they linked up with in the parking lot. They stood at the front, casing the scene. It was dark inside, and the dance floor was even darker, illuminated only by the dim glow lights that hung overhead. The only legitimate lighting was at the concession stand and the dining area that sat to their right. The arcade was illuminated as well, but not as bright.

Sparkles was already turnt. Huncho looked around in search of familiar faces, sweeping the arcade to see if anyone he knew was posted at the pool table. It was packed and full of a lot more activity than usual, but there was no sign of anyone he knew. All around, guys were stuntin' their freshest fits and females were rockin' tank and halter tops to go with their most provocative booty shorts.

Flame tapped Huncho's arm and pointed to the back of the club in the right-hand corner. "There go Jayvo an' them, right there."

Triggadale

Huncho looked to see Jayvo posted with ten other Mafiosos. Among them were several females. Some were straight-up groupies while others were part of the female branch of the Mafia: Southside Queens.

They made their way to the back, walking along the sideline. Flame looked into the crowded dance floor as they passed by. Females were twerkin' like it was their last night to party while others were dancing with their homegirls.

Knuck If You Buck came on, and a train of young hooligans bounced around slamming their fists into their palms. They all wore green. Flame locked eyes with one of them: a tall, muscular guy who was a lighter shade of brown. He rocked Mad Max dreads, barely to his neck, and on his face was a devilish grin. They held each other's gaze until the train passed by.

Flame looked over his shoulder at them. Hit Squad Taliban. They weren't from Clayton County, but neither were a lot of people present, cliques especially. They were from the Southside, yes, but they were from College Park.

They reached Jayvo, and Huncho dapped him up along with the other present Mafiosos. Flame, Silencer, and Big B did the same. They posted up, and thirty minutes later the Mafia was deep. All night they put on. Ski pulled up two hours before midnight with Baby D, both Mafiosos. They got the DJ to spin their songs and piped up as everyone got hype to their tunes.

Everyone except Hit Squad Taliban, that is. They were posted off to the side, muggin', and to the side is where they stayed until the lights came on at closing time.

Huncho, Flame, and Ski had wandered to the concession stand to grab a few cans of Crunk Juice before the ride home, and now were headed outside together. The crowd was thick, slowly filing out of the exit into the chilly night. Ski tried in vain to peer over the crowd to the door in search of the rest of the Mafia. Flame shook his head at his attempt. On his tiptoes, he came to Flame's chest. Ski brushed his hand over his curly head. It was useless.

"Man, fuck that shit." Ski turned around and looked up. "Aye, Huncho, where y'all headed when y'all leave here?" he yelled above the loud and over-excited crowd.

"If it wasn't so late, we'd tie yo' black, obese ass up and shoot to the barbershop."

Flame brought his fist to his mouth. "Ow." Blessed with a good grade of hair, Ski had to get a fresh chop every other week to keep it low, as he preferred. It was a task he often let slip due to his preoccupation with the streets. He shrugged. "Y'all just mad 'cause all the hos got crunk when my verse came on."

Flame sucked his teeth. "Boy, stop!"

"Stop what? You know my shit snappin'!"

"To who? You?"

"Naw, nigga. To everybody." A light-skinned guy with waves bumped into Ski. He spazzed and pushed him into the crowd. "Fuck up off me, man! You trippin'! Steppin' all on a nigga shoes and shit!"

Huncho ran his fingers back through his dreads, then shook them. "Shid, we 'bout get something to eat, then head over to The Spot. Why, what's up?"

"We headed the same way," Ski said. "Shoota got a couple freaks on deck we finna run through, so y'all betta come on with us if y'all tryna get it."

"A'ight, let's do it."

Huncho was about to say something to Flame when a short, thick redbone female ran up crying and screaming. "They out there jumping on Nard!" she yelled in a panic.

Nard belonged to Southside Mafia, so at the mention of him being in some drama, there wasn't much to talk about. "Where he at?" Huncho said.

"Come on!" she yelled.

Huncho, Flame, and Ski pushed their way through the crowd behind her. By the time they made it to the parking lot, Nard was leaning up against a burgundy Honda Civic, badly banged up with his shirt ripped and one of his shoes missing. People and cars filled the parking lot. It was so jam-packed it was hard to single anybody out. Everybody looked suspect.

The girl who had come for help began pointing people out. "That's one of them, right there," she said. "Him, too. The one with the green on." Everyone she pointed out was either wearing green or rockin' green bandanas to signify their affiliation to Hit Squad Taliban.

"That's them Squad niggas!" Flame said.

"Fuck-niggas!" Huncho growled, face twisted in a scowl. He was livid. Nard's assault was an assault on his ego. Nobody bombed on the Mafia. Nobody! Especially in Riverdale. Somebody had to pay. He cut across the crowded parking lot, headed to his car. Trunk popped, he leaned in and came up holding a 12-gauge. He chambered a round and held it down to the side of his leg as he speed-walked toward the part of the lot where Hit Squad Taliban was posted. His mind had gone blank. Laughter, music, and conversation faded.

More Mafia members were walking up, ready to aid Nard. Their numbers grew so fast Flame hadn't noticed Huncho creep away. When he looked around and didn't spot him, he hit him on his Metro, but Huncho didn't answer.

"Ski, you seen Huncho?" Flame asked.

"Shid, goddamn." Ski looked left to right. "He was just standin' right there."

Three quick booms went off, causing the parking lot to erupt in panic. Huncho had walked up on the group of H.S.T. members huddled around two cars that were backed in. Without hesitation he'd opened fire. The first shot hit the H.S.T. affiliate in the chest, knocking him off his feet. He lay sprawled out on the pavement, blood gushing. The other two shots were directed at the fleeing crowd that tried

13

to escape. Buckshot pellets sprayed their legs and face, but none were fatal like the first blast.

Huncho finished emptying the pump and ran. He was met by Ski, who took the pump from him and passed it to a female. "Here, put this in your car and get the fuck out of here!" he said.

A Southside Queen, she did as she was told with no questions asked. Pump in hand, she hopped in the backseat of a sky-blue Camry driven by another female. She ducked low between the seats as the driver crunk the car and rode off.

Huncho tossed Flame the keys to his Charger and jumped in the trunk of another car driven by yet another female. She drove off and blended in with traffic on Highway 85, riding right past the police.

Huncho arrived safely at 7675 Lyle Drive, a block located in Riverdale off S.R. 138, and was greeted with love by more than twenty Mafiosos.

At the same time on the other side of town, Hit Squad Taliban was mourning their loss and plotting revenge. A war had just begun, and the once-sedate atmosphere of Riverdale was about to enter a new era.

Chapter 1

Huncho was on his phone in the living room, laid back on the tan, faux-leather loveseat. Sitting adjacent to his right was a matching sofa, and to his left a recliner to complete the set. At the sofa and loveseat's far sides were granite end tables, and at the core of the room was a glass top coffee table with granite legs. Having pulled two chairs in from the back patio, Slap-Rocks and Shoota sat in front of the television playing Madden on the Xbox.

It had been a few days since the shooting at Sparkles that left one dead and several injured. Huncho had been under the radar since the incident, but he was far from inconvenienced. Everything from weed to females was at his fingertips. The Mafia made sure he was comfortable and wanted for nothing while he lay low.

His description had been given at the scene of the murder, but a tall, slim, black male with blonde-tip dreads in all black could be anyone. Needless to say, he wasn't worried much. His only concern was his name being implicated by the streets or by some loose lips inside his own clique. People had a tendency to brag about what one of their homeboys did, not realizing that was the closest thing to dry snitching, because when one person tells another, the story continues to get told until the wrong person hears it. That was his main reason for laying low.

Huncho was seventeen and troublesome. He went to Riverdale High School, but dropped out last year in '04 after repeating the ninth grade twice. When he broke the news to his mother, she snapped and kicked him out. Like he cared. He didn't really fuck with her like that, anyways. All she was good for was getting drunk and taking her resentment for his father out on him. Subsequently, he'd been on his own since he was sixteen.

For six months he bounced house-to-house, crashing at different homeboys' cribs and kicking doors until some guys on the block took a liking to him and stamped him Southside Mafia. From there, Huncho took off building a name within the ranks, getting in on some major moves. With no other family outside of his deadbeat mother, Southside Mafia was his family. When the old heads who stamped him Mafia went down for robbing a pawn shop, he stepped up to the plate. A couple months later he got a crib on Lyle Drive and labeled it The Spot for any Mafioso to kick-it at any time. With Flame as his ace, he was holdin' it down, but they weren't the only ones going hard, by far.

Huncho laughed. At the dining room table, Tee was putting micros in Yana's head. Weave and hair care products littered the table's surface. Flame and a group of Mafiosos were smoking weed and shooting dice in the kitchen. The cream apartment walls appeared white from the marijuana smoke.

A knock at the door snapped everyone to attention. Tee and Yana were staring at the door, the dice game stopped, and Huncho was no longer focused on his phone conversation. Shoota lifted a sofa cushion and grabbed the Choppa. Huncho looked up at Flame, who was already headed to the door with a 9mm in hand. He peeked through the curtain, opened the door, and stepped aside to let two females in carrying McDonald's bags. Seeing that they were Queens, everyone carried on.

The first female, a brown-skinned, 5-foot-6, 135 pound beauty named Daja, wore her hair in braids. Missy was the second girl. She was not much to look at, but dedicated to the cause. She was skinny, no ass, no breasts, no nothing.

Daja walked across the living room, sat on Huncho's lap, and started feeding him french fries from her bag. She was the one who drove him from Sparkles the night of the shooting. She showed no resistance as Huncho rubbed her

16

ass through the Baby Phat jeans that looked to have been painted on her.

Get off the phone, she mouthed, knowing more than likely he was talking to his baby mama or some other female. He smiled and held up his finger. Moments later he was hanging up.

Daja pulled food from one of the bags. "I got you a quarter pounder with cheese. I couldn't remember what you wanted, and you wouldn't answer the phone when I called." She handed him his food. "Missy got your drank in her bag."

Huncho unwrapped the quarter pounder and took a bite. "'Preciate that, shawdy."

"Oh yeah, we bumped into ol' lame-ass Gotti at the Get-N-Go on Riverdale Road."

"Gotti?" Huncho's brow creased. "Who the fuck is Gotti?"

"You remember, the nigga that checked Tall-Teezee at that house party in Lovejoy."

"Oh yeah. What about him, though?"

"He ran up on us talkin' 'bout the Squad gon' get ya boy for what he did. So I'm like, 'you trippin', what you talkin 'bout?'"

Huncho sat up, and Daja slid off his lap to his side.

"Then he started talkin' 'bout they know who killed Taliban at Sparkles the other night, and they lookin' for his ass. I just told him I don't know what he talkin' 'bout and kept it movin'."

Huncho laughed and stuck a few fries in his mouth. "Aye, Flame, you hear this shit shawdy just said?"

"Man, fuck them niggas. They don't want no smoke," Flame said, unconcerned.

They continued to talk until they finished eating, then Huncho and Daja went to one of the bedrooms, smoked a blunt, and fucked for an hour before falling asleep. Huncho woke up to an empty bed. He looked out the window to

17

find the sun had set. He scratched at an itch in his dreads, got up, and made his way to the living room. There were Mafiosos lounging around half-asleep, a cloud of smoke lingering in the air. Flame was lying on the long sofa with a AK-47 laid across his lap, an extra hundred-round clip on the coffee table. Everywhere he looked there was a gun in sight.

He smiled. "These niggas trained to go."

The sanctuary of Hattie G. Watkins Memorial Chapel was indeed a somber scene. People, both young and grown, littered the pews, and a line of mourners formed a loop from back to front. Today was Taliban's wake, and friends and family were gathered to pay their last respects. H.S.T. members had respected him so much they had donned him *Taliban* for being a walking definition of the movement.

Everyone seemed to have been snatched straight from their own definition of what their reality deemed "the usual." Some were dressed up while others were dressed casually. *R.I.P. Taliban* shirts with a picture of Taliban on the front were being rocked by Squad affiliates, who were noticeably present and scattered throughout the room one of which was Dre, Taliban's twin brother.

At the foot of the altar, Taliban's body rested in a black casket surrounded by flowers, beside which was a large photograph of him smiling. Aside from condolences and the consoling reassurances offered amongst kin, no one spoke. The quiet sobs and shuffling feet of loved ones across the lavender carpet was all there was to be heard. It was obvious everyone present was feeling the loss. So many had come to show their support, and as Dre stared down the rows of faces seated in the pews as he shuffled towards the altar, he found comfort in this, however minimal it was. On the front pew was his little sister and mother, a short, graceful woman clad in an all-black dress. Her onyx skin tone made her bloodshot eyes all the more

18

conspicuous, and as he watched, a lone tear slid down her cheek.

The line came to a stop when he stood before the casket, looking down at his brother. He couldn't shake the feeling he was attending his own funeral. Identical twins, they both were black and tall with stout builds, low cuts, and light brown eyes.

Dre had already declared death on the ones responsible and anyone who was kin or affiliated with them. Taliban was more than his brother, they were best friends. Everything they did, they did so together. Had Marko not tackled him to the ground, they probably would've died together. It had been so close that a split second's hesitance would've meant him in a suit and matching casket sitting adjacent to where he now stood.

By time he looked up, the shooter was running the opposite way. He started to give chase, but stopped at the sight of his brother lying on the ground and clutching his chest, blood spilling from his mouth. He rushed to his side, lifted him up, and looked him in his eyes until the life left them.

Born and raised on The Grove, he was no stranger to the pain that accompanied the death of someone close. Shock. Disbelief. The helplessness that followed. Empty voids that left him numb to the core. Tears. All that, and still nothing could've prepared him for what he now felt. Distraught? Enraged? No, this was something else entirely. A feeling beyond words.

"We gon' get them niggas, bra," someone whispered in his ear. He draped an arm over his shoulders in a consoling manner. "Don't e'en sweat it. We gon' get 'em."

The voice registered and Dre realized it was his homeboy Gotti, a major face in the Squad. He was a lighter shade of brown and wore his hair in a Mad Max. Tall and muscular in build, he had punched out his share of Mafiosos.

Dre nodded, trying to shake the ominous feeling, but it was as if he was looking into a mirror. He shook his head in anguish. Things would never be the same. He stared at his brother, transfixed until Gotti prodded him, then they made their way to the door. Outside, they stopped at the top of the stairs. The sky was gray, their bandanas were green, and inside they were feeling blue.

Dre reached into the pocket of his baggy blue jeans and removed a cigarette from a pack of Newports. Putting a lighter to its tip, he took a deep pull, savoring the taste of tobacco in his mouth as homicidal thoughts permeated his mind. Exhaling a cloud of smoke, he walked to the side of the church and Gotti following. H.S.T. members stood around talking in hushed tones. At his approach, they ceased.

He stood beside his most loyal friend, Tevo, who was light-skinned and slightly taller in stature. With his wavy hair one might take him as a pretty boy, but he could get down with the best of them, a fact he'd proven many times. From King Road to Jackson Landing, he'd earned his place as a certified Grove Street official.

"This shit fucked up, bra." Dre hit the cigarette. "My nigga, I'm finna go ham on these niggas, shawdy."

"I feel ya, bra. You know I'm with ya," Tevo said.

"Ain't nobody found out where them niggas be at?" Dre asked.

"Naw, but everybody sayin' it was some Southside Mafia nigga named Huncho," Tevo said.

"Yeah, I done heard the nigga name before in the street. I think it was some li'l bitch I was fuckin' with talkin' 'bout the nigga, but I can't remember who the fuck it was," Dre said, trying his damnedest to remember.

"I heard them niggas be at Club Chocolate on the east side sometimes, and over there at 20 Grand off Old Nat," a jet-black, plait-wearing Squad member named Marko said.

It was he who had tackled Dre to the ground the night of Taliban's murder.

Dre nodded, taking a long pull on the Newport. As he exhaled, he saw his mother and sister approaching from across the gloomy, semi-full parking lot. He thumped the cigarette away out of respect for his mother, stepped out from the crowd to meet her, and took her into his embrace. Releasing her, he stooped down to hug his sister. They were all he had left of his immediate family. He stood and faced his mother.

"Dre, I see all y'all done gathered up over here, and I came to tell you don't get yourself in no trouble over this mess. Ain't nothing you can do to bring your brother back." She preached loud enough for the others to hear, also. "God called his name, and now he's in a better place with no worries. So, my advice to you and your friends is to just let the good Lord handle it, and he'll punish the one responsible for taking Deontae away from us."

Dre stared off, unable to look his mother in her eyes. "We straight, Ma. We ain't gon' get in no trouble."

The following day, Riverdale Road, also known as Grove Street, saw more traffic than usual. A majority of the traffic was family members coming to and from Dre's mother's house where most of the funeral attendees had gathered for dinner.

While the family ate and congregated, Hit Squad Taliban sat in the backyard of Gotti's one-story, three-bedroom house off Crystal Lake Drive talking about Southside Mafia, number one on their shit list. "What we gon' do is split up and hit both spots," Dre said. "If you see them niggas, bomb on they ass! But if that nigga Huncho wit' 'em, just chill. Call me. I want him for myself."

"My sister went to Riverdale Middle School with his right-hand," Cap said. "Say she know him."

"She know where he stay?" Dre asked.

21

"I got her on that now."

"Get in touch with her and see what's up. See what she done found out," Dre said before resuming conversation with the group.

Dre wasn't the leader of Hit Squad, nor was he the oldest. In fact, there was no leader. Everyone was their own man in the Squad, but at nineteen, Dre was well respected due to the work he put in for even the newest faces of the clique. The Grove had mad love for Dre and Taliban, so for many, this was personal.

By the time the sun set, they were amped and ready to ride. Twelve cars deep, they pulled out, heading for the clubs in search of Huncho and other Southside Mafiosos. Before they hit any club scene, though, they made one stop.

Flame's mother's house was shot up, riddled with over sixty bullet holes.

Chapter 2

Camry was on the couch watching a reality show in the living room of her mother's house in King's Manor, a huge stone and granite structure off Taylor Road. She'd planned to go out and party, but decided against it after succumbing to nausea and throwing up a few times. Pregnant, her intentions were to enjoy her last days of independence, because once she started showing it was a wrap, and a double wrap when she had the baby. Her mother had already made it clear she wouldn't be babysitting. All the same, she was in for the night. She released a sigh of frustration and began flicking through the channels.

Going out was quickly becoming something of the past. Her pregnancy wouldn't allow it, and once she delivered, she knew her baby's daddy wasn't going to babysit while she hung out. More than likely he'd be doing the same thing he was doing now. Running the streets.

Camry was a sixteen-year-old junior at Riverdale High School. She met her baby's daddy at Kendrick Middle School three years ago when she was a cheerleader and he played small forward for the school basketball team. She wasn't a groupie like most of the cheerleading squad who threw themselves at the starters. Standing 5-foot-5 with butter-soft skin, long, shapely legs and shoulder-length hair the color of autumn maple leaves, she was more of the conservative type. As a result, she wasn't approached as often as her peers who constantly advertised the benefits of flattering them.

Then one night after a game against Pointe South Middle School, he approached her asking for her number. Not wanting to become another name on his long list of sexual conquest, she denied his request, and from then until a year ago, they were nothing more than cordial associates.

What brought them together was their Physical Science teacher's attempt to help him pull his grades up by offering her extra credit to tutor him. Many times the subject would go from Science to more personal topics where she got to learn a lot about this guy she had labeled bad news, and pretty soon she found herself with a whole new perspective of him. Misunderstood.

They became close friends, and she wanted so badly to be the one to change him. Eventually the sex just came out of nowhere. Unlike the way he did most girls, though, he didn't broadcast it. He even made their relationship official by asking her out. She knew he still did his thing, or so she'd heard, but she made the mistake many young girls had made before her. She had fallen in love with a street nigga.

Not long afterward he dropped out of school, got in the Mafia, and got his own crib. After telling her mother she was staying at her best friend Yummy's house a few times, only to spend the weekend with him while Yummy covered for her, she ended up pregnant.

As she flicked through the channels, *Bossy* by Kelis blared from her phone. It was the ringtone she had programmed for Yummy. With a huff, she raised the phone to her ear, and continued channel surfing. She knew more than likely Yummy was calling to see if she was still going out, and she resented it.

She sighed. "Yeah?"

"Bitch, get ya ass up. I got somethin' to tell you," Yummy said. "You woke?"

"Yes, I'm woke. I answered the phone, didn't I?"

"Well, girl, Melody just called me and said somebody shot up Flame mama's house, and everybody sayin' it got somethin' to do with what happened at Sparkles the other night." Yummy popped her gum. "But get this. She said everybody sayin' Huncho the one that did the shooting, and

24

it was one of them Hit Squad Taliban dudes he killed. Now they lookin' for him, too."

"Why they puttin' Daldrick's name in stuff? That boy ain't killed nobody!" Camry said. Daldrick was Huncho's real name. Camry never addressed him by his alias.

Yummy sucked her teeth. "Well, that's what everybody sayin'."

Camry returned the gesture. "Did anybody get shot at Flame's mama's house?"

"I don't know. They say it sounded like a machine gun was goin' off or somethin'. It's, like, hella police over there right now. A helicopter and all."

"I wonder if he know yet?"

"I don't know, but is you goin' out with us tonight? Amanda got her mama's car, and we're goin' to 20 Grand."

"I'm not feelin' good," Camry said, "but let me call you back. I need to call and check on my baby."

They ended the call and Camry dialed Huncho's number by memory. He answered on the third ring, saying he was at the studio with his homeboys. They had a local hit song called *Knock His Ass Out*. She told him what had happened at Flame's house and his attitude changed. He ended the call without so much as a 'bye' or 'I'll call you back.'

She lay her phone down, feeling as though she'd made a mistake by telling him what she heard. Huncho and Flame were like brothers. They were down for each other like four flats on a box Chevy. That in mind, there was no doubt in her heart where Huncho was headed that very moment.

***

Flame ran down Scott Road, clutching the pistol on his waist to keep it from sliding down his pant leg. Up ahead he could see the flashing red and blue lights, but he cared nothing about a police presence. His family's safety was all that mattered. As he got closer, he could see his mother talking to a short, fat, middle-aged detective and a uniform officer while she held his baby brother and little sister close to her side.

He tried to get through the yellow crime scene tape and was met by a tall, stocky, dark-skinned Clayton County police officer. "You can't cross this line. This is a crime scene," the officer said with authority.

"Man, that's my mama's house," Flame yelled. "I gotta check on my family!"

Flame's mother heard him and told the officer in front of her, a bald, ex-military-looking white guy in his late thirties. He walked over to where Flame was arguing with the other officer and told him to let him in. Reluctantly, the officer raised the strip of yellow tape and allowed Flame to pass. He mean-mugged him and went over to his family. Seeing tears in his mother's eyes, he did a quick headcount of his loved ones.

"Ma, you a'ight?"

"Baby, they shot up the house!" she cried. "What have you gotten into?"

Flame's face screwed up immediately. "I ain't did nothin', Mama. I just got over here when I got the call."

"Son, I'd like to ask you a few questions." It was the detective his mother had been talking to. "Now, if you know who's responsible for this, you need to let me know, because the next time your family might not be so lucky."

Flame spun around with a quickness. "Man, look, I wasn't here, a'ight? I don't know who did it."

For the next ten minutes he answered a series of questions from the detectives. Questions to which he gave equivocal answers.

After the questioning, the police left and he called Huncho and Ski, who weren't far away. They had come while he was being questioned by the detectives. Seeing the police, they pulled into the driveway of another Mafioso down the street and watched the scene from a distance. They answered and told him to walk down the street to meet them.

Upon his arrival, Huncho's face was etched in genuine concern. "Everything straight, bra?"

"Yeah, shawdy. Mama trippin', though. She blamin' me for the shit. I just got kicked out."

"Shid, boy, you know the Mafia got ya," Huncho said.

"Who you think did the shit, though?" Ski said. "That's what I wanna know."

"Them fuck-ass Taliban niggas, who else?" Flame spit in the grass.

Huncho nodded. "So you know what the business is, then, right?"

"Hell yeah. Shid, it's guns up!"

They hopped in the car and headed to 4900 Block to comb the streets near Grove Street and Godby Road, looking for anyone who even looked like they were affiliated with H.S.T.

Unsuccessful, they retreated back to The Spot.

***

The lights came on and the DJ stopped the music as bottles and chairs flew through the air. 20 Grand looked like a WWF WrestleMania match as the two cliques went at it. Hit Squad Taliban was outnumbered four-to-one and was catching the worst end of the battle.

8800 Block and 7675 were forty deep and riding to the fullest. Fulton County Police and club security rushed in, spraying pepper spray to clear the club and break up the fights, but they only succeeded in pushing the rumble to the parking lot.

People ran for their cars while others continued fighting or tried to catch their breath, coughing and choking from the pepper spray. An H.S.T. member named T.O. Green was the first to his car. He pulled a .45 from under the seat and fired shots into the crowd, hitting a Southside Queen in the leg and an 8800 Mafioso in the arm.

The first shots fired set off a chain reaction, and the sound of gunfire erupted all over the parking lot. Female screams could be heard along with sirens, slamming doors, and blaring car horns. A helicopter hovered above, shining a spotlight on the parking lot as Fulton County Police flooded the scene like a disturbed ant bed. By the time they got things under control three people had been shot, several were injured, and thirteen arrests where made.

Dre was on I-20 on his way to Club Chocolate when he got the call from Tevo informing him Southside Mafia was at 20 Grand. He was fuming, furious he hadn't followed his first mindset and pulled up at 20 Grand instead of Club Chocolate. Hearing how the Squad was outnumbered, he grew even more angry.

"Was that nigga Huncho there?" he asked.

"Naw, bra. And if he was, I didn't see him."

"My nigga, I'm murkin' them niggas on sight, shawdy!" Dre hung up and slammed his fist into the steering wheel. "Fuck!"

***

Detective Ellis, a middle-aged black man, stood behind a tall wood podium at the front of the room. Downloaded MySpace pictures of Southside Mafia were being displayed from a projector on the wall beside him. Facing a group of officers seated at the long table in the center of the room, he addressed the problem at hand.

"They are said to have started in 2003 and quickly grew in numbers. It's believed two sets or chapters, as well as a female branch, make up the gang. Our Gang Task Force has gathered some information and has been able to put some names with the different sets."

The officers in the briefing room paid close attention, some taking notes as he spoke. They were part of a special task force put together to bring the gang activity to an end. After the arrests made from the incident at 20 Grand they gained a lot of information, some of it about Taliban's murder.

Ellis was an ex-Navy Seal. He was hell-bent on becoming the Chief of Police. He saw the gang crisis as an opportunity to advance his credentials, which is why he had volunteered to head the task force.

"The two sectors believed to make up the Southside Mafia street gang are 7675 and 8800," he continued. "Then there's Southside Queens, the females."

"Uh, excuse me, Detective Ellis." A young, white detective named Foster had his hand slightly raised, pen ready. "You said they were believed to have originated in 2003. Do we have any intel on it's originators or possibly how they were formed?"

Ellis cleared his throat. "As far as we know right now, they started off as a rap group. The founders have yet to be confirmed. Most of these young gangbangers rarely know the history of what they are claiming and ready to kill and die for. But, as of now, we believe they started as a rap group."

Foster scribbled some notes and looked back up. "And their origin, where were they started? Did they come from out of town like the Bloods and Crips?"

"Uh, no. Unfortunately they were started right up under our nose." The projector went to the next slide. It showed a group of dread-head teens in black tees, flashing guns and throwing up the *M*s. Ellis stepped from behind the podium and walked closer to the image. "Southside Mafia is all over the Southside, though we do know that 8800 is upper

Riverdale Road and 7675 was originated on a street off
S.R. 138. A Lyle Drive, I believe."

"Detective Ellis," an attractive, Asian female detective
called out. "Is there any connection with Southside Mafia
to the Mafia in Macon, Georgia?"

"All possibilities are being investigated at this time, but
in my opinion, no. And it's highly unlikely."

Detective Ellis continued to bring the special task force
up to speed with his knowledge of the Mafia. When the
meeting was over, they all went their separate ways with
the information they had collected. They were all surprised
at how quickly the gang was gaining notoriety and literally
flourishing out of nowhere, unlike Hit Squad Taliban, a
gang they began hearing about as early as 1998.

The special task force had set up meetings with the
local schools and monitored MySpace pages. The schools
had become recruiting grounds, and the more who joined
either gang, the bolder their acts became. There were gang
fights in the hallways of the schools, some involving as
many as thirty students. After football games there were
fights that led to shootouts in the parking lot, and it seemed
as if the police had no control of the situation. Both gangs
had no fear of rivals or the police.

"So, what are we going to do about this Huncho guy?"
a detective named Jones asked. "His name has popped up
several times about the murder."

"We don't have enough on him yet to arrest him," Ellis
said. "We don't even know his real name. All we have is
the name Huncho and a bunch of secondhand information.
None of the ones we talked to actually saw the shooting.
They're going off what they heard in the streets."

"True, but the streets talk," Jones said. "So, more than
likely he's our man."

"Yeah, but we still need a witness."

Chapter 3

It was a sunny Saturday afternoon, and Huncho, Flame, and Ski were walking through Southlake Mall after picking up the customized hats and shirts they had made. A couple weeks had passed since the last run in with H.S.T. Since then, both the Mafia and the Squad had been on the news. Pictures of some of the members posing with AK-47's and various handguns were being shown on every news channel in hopes of discouraging affiliation, but it only added to their notoriety. The beef was now the talk of the city. From Tara Boulevard to Old National Highway, it seemed like everybody wanted to be a part of it.

"Ain't yo' name Huncho?" a slim female with braids asked as they sat in the food court eating American Deli hot wings.

Huncho bit into a wing and began chewing. "Depends on who wanna know."

"My friend over there wants your number." She tossed her head back in her friend's direction. "She said she wanna holla at you."

Huncho looked over at three other girls sitting a couple of tables away. "Which one you talkin' 'bout?"

"The red one with the long hair. Her name Shea," she said. "And, um, ain't you in Southside Mafia?"

"Tell your friend to come over and holla at me," Huncho replied with a smile, ignoring her question. He was stuck on Shea. *Shawdy kinda thick*, he thought.

"Shid," Flame said as she started to walk off. "Matter fact, why don't all y'all come over here and chill with us?"

The other females came over and joined them at the table. Thirty minutes later they were leaving the mall to hit The Spot. Shea rode with Huncho and Ski. Flame hopped in a black Honda Accord with the other girls and followed. At The Spot, the girls were fascinated by the Mafia and the way they rolled. To their adolescent minds, they seemed to know how to have fun. Money. Weed. Cars. Metros. The customized attire they wore to represent. The vibe was enticing and made them want to be a part of it. Get lost in it, even. At least this was how the Mafia perceived it.

Blunts were fired up back-to-back, and next came the beer and liquor. Before the girls realized what hit them, they were in separate rooms lying across the bed naked. The Mafia ran trains on them, making them a part of the clique for the night.

Ski took the keys to the Honda, then he and Huncho peeled off. By time the girls awoke, sick and sore from all the fucking, it was past midnight. Shea was the first to emerge from the room. The house was more crowded than it had been earlier, and as she looked around, she took in all the new faces. The music was loud, and as usual, smoke filled the living room. In the midst of everything she spotted one of her friends asleep on the couch with her pants unbuttoned. She went back in the room she came from and began searching for her purse and phone. Finding them and seeing the time, she rushed back into the living room to the couch and shook her friend in a panic.

"Zaria! Zaria, wake up. Where's Brandi and Meeka at?"

Zaria stirred, unconcerned. "I don't know."

"They in the back sleep, shawdy," Shoota said.

"Well, can you go get them for me? 'Cause we gotta go." Shea looked around. "And where's Huncho?"

"He had to run somewhere." Shoota was twisting one of his dreads. "He'll be back in a minute."

All the girls were up and gathered in the living room when Huncho and Ski came through the door, laughing. They had been out joyriding in the car the girls came in.

Shea was trying to talk to Huncho as if she was his girl, but he was ignoring her. She asked when she could see him again, and he busted out laughing. "What's so funny about that?" she asked.

Triggadale

You just sucked and fucked all my homeboys like it's all good, he thought. He decided to save her the embarrassment. "Shawdy, you trippin', but I'll holla."

After a few more minutes of conversation, the girls left. What Huncho didn't know is Shea knew Camry. Being from Garden Walk, he assumed she went to North Clayton High School.

For the next few days she called him nonstop until he just stopped answering her calls. At that, she began texting him threats and leaving all types of crazy messages on his voicemail.

It wasn't until she threatened to tell Camry they had fucked that he responded. He sent her a text saying he wanted to see her. He told her to meet him in Alexander Falls, off Lake Ridge Parkway, but when she reached the location he wasn't there. Instead, she was greeted by six Southside Queens. They beat her down in the parking lot, stomping her out while Huncho stood up the street, watching from a distance.

Later that same night, Shea was talking on the phone to one of the many people who had heard what happened to her. She was telling them what happened and why, leaving out how she and her homegirls got freaked out at The Spot. She was making it seem as if she and Huncho had been seeing each other on some I-love-you-boyfriend-girlfriend type shit.

"Girl, I can't stand his ass. I got something for that nigga, though," she said. "You know my homegirl Brandi be fuckin' with them Hit Squad Taliban niggas, right?"

"Ain't they beefin' or somethin'?" the girl on the other end of the phone asked.

"Yeah, and it's because Huncho is supposed to have killed one of their homeboys at Sparkles," Shea said. "Matta fact, let me call you back. This Brandi on my other line."

33

It was a cool night on Battle Creek Road, and Tara Stadium was packed with a rowdy crowd. North Clayton was playing Riverdale High School in football, and the score was tied at 21 in the fourth quarter. North Clayton and Riverdale had always been rival schools, so both were trying to pull the game off and come out as winners.

The bleachers were thick on both sides, and the competition on the field was intense. Both teams' cheerleaders were hyped in an attempt to motivate the players to victory. The Raider, Riverdale's mascot, was doing the Lean-With-It-Rock-With-It.

"Aye, shawdy, them Mafia niggas here," Tevo told Dre as they chilled in the stands.

Dre nodded. "You strapped?"

Tevo lifted his shirt to reveal the black .45 on his waist. "Nigga, you know I keep my bitch with me!"

"After the game."

For the remainder of the game they chilled and called up more H.S.T. affiliates. The side of Clayton County they were on was Mafia turf, but they were toting hardware to equalize the battle. Dre hadn't come to fight, anyway. He wanted to kill as many Mafiosos as possible until he got to Huncho for killing his brother. Whatever it took to get to him, he was willing to do it.

Riverdale won by a touchdown, and as they left the stadium, the crowd was hype. Football players and band members loaded onto the buses that lined the sidewalk. Parents hurried across the parking lot to their cars, anxious to escape the rowdy crowd of youth. The Clayton County Police were present, but there were nowhere near enough to control the crowd. They were mostly there to direct the traffic.

Students posted at the mouth of the exit gate looked up. Commotion was brewing. From the curb out front of the

34

stadium, a brown-skin student glanced in the gates' direction and did a double-take. Something was about to go down. Sensing a scene unfolding, he tapped his friend and pointed.

Brandi was skip-walking through the crowd, fists balled at her sides. Behind her Shea, Meka, Zaria, and a few other females from The Grove weaved through the crowded stadium with just as much purpose. Still salty about Shea's beat down, they were on a mission. Brandi's eyes scanned the crowd from behind until she spotted her target exiting the stadium gate. Determined to catch her, she broke into a jog.

Almost to the parking lot, Brandi came up fast behind her. Just as she thought, Daja was solo. Without warning, she cocked back and swung a mean right hook, rocking her in the jaw mid-step. The crowd hooted and hollered as Daja stumbled left, head-first toward the pavement.

Brandi tied her braids back and charged. Daja caught herself and spun around to swing, but she was too slow. Brandi was all over her. The other Grove Street females jumped in, swinging and clawing at Daja like savages. Outnumbered, she dropped her head, flinging wild windmill punches in a desperate attempt to defend herself. The crowd gathered closer to witness the ass whoopin'.

Latching onto Daja's braids, Shea began yanking her head around, slinging her about as Meka hooked her mid-section with uppercuts, and everyone else continued raining down blows. Daja stopped swinging and gripped her braids, vying for control as her body shifted from left to right. Relentlessly they continued to pound away until she hit the ground and balled up in a fetal position.

Football players and band members hung from the bus windows, rooting as they began stomping her out.

"Shawdy, look at that shit!" Marko pointed at the brawl as him, Dre, Tevo, and Gotti walked out of the stadium exit gates, headed to the car. "Them hos goin' off over there!"

35

Tevo climbed on top of a powder-blue Honda Civic and stood on the hood to get a better view. "That's Meka and them, ain't it?"

Southside Queens ran to Daja's rescue, rushing into the brawl swinging and pulling hair in an attempt to save her from the beat down. Katrina punched Shea in the mouth, busting her lip. Shea snapped and took off on Katrina. Meka had Tee in a headlock while Brandi pummeled her face. Daja hopped up and unleashed a fury of punches on one of the Grove Street females while Shea and Katrina continue to go at it. Zaria blindsided Katrina, dropping her in the middle of the parking lot.

"Beat them hos' ass!" Ski yelled from the surrounding crowd. Huncho and several other Mafiosos flanked him on both sides. "Represent for that M.A.F.I.A, shawdy!"

One of the girls had her shirt and bra ripped off, exposing her boobs. The crowd went wild, but even that didn't stop them. Some of the girls squared off and went toe-to-toe like niggas in a boxing match while some tugged at each other's hair, slinging each other around until finally the police arrived and broke them up.

As the crowd dispersed, Tevo caught sight of a familiar face walking, arm draped over the shoulder of a thick, dark chocolate female with honey-blonde highlights. He locked in on him as everyone spread out, just to be sure. Catching a better glimpse of him as the crowd shifted, he was positive.

He tapped Dre's rib with his elbow. "Oh, shit! Yo, Dre, that's Huncho right there! Look, in the crowd with the thick, dark-skin chick. See 'im?"

Dre searched frantically, eyes shifting back and forth throughout the crowd until at last he was staring at the one responsible for taking the life of his other half. His temples began to pulse as his teeth clenched and unclenched. He spun on his heels and shot to his pearl-white Malibu. Popping the driver side door, he grabbed his Glock 40 from under the seat, racking one into the chamber. He looked back to where he had spotted Huncho and searched the crowd.

Tevo, Gotti, and Marko made it to the car just as he caught sight of Huncho once again. He had crossed the parking lot and was almost to the street. Dre rushed around to the passenger side.

Tevo raised his arms, lost. "What you doin'?"

Dre tossed him the car keys and pointed toward the street. "Follow him!"

Dre hopped in on the passenger side. Tevo got in the driver's seat, and Marko and Gotti climbed in the back. Tevo crunk the car up, backed out, and pulled into traffic.

"Tevo, man, I'm finna murk this nigga, shawdy." Dre stared ahead, expressionless. "Don't let him get away!"

Tevo eased to a stop at the parking lot entrance, awaiting the right of way to pull off. The traffic on Battle Creek Road was gridlocked, and people were everywhere, walking along the sidewalk, darting in between cars, screaming and yelling at passing vehicles while the car horns of Riverdale students honked in celebration of their victory.

Pressed for time, Tevo swerved onto the road, stealing a spot in the congested traffic. Dre stared straight ahead into the night as they eased up the street.

"Can you still see the nigga?" He was shifting in his seat, trying to get a better view. It was getting hard to keep Huncho in sight through the crowd.

"Not no more."

"Man, fuck this shit! This nigga ain't gettin' away this time." Dre opened the door and got out. "Meet me up the street," he yelled over his shoulder.

Dre joined the crowd on the sidewalk and speed-walked, eyes ahead in search of Huncho. As he walked, memories flashed through his mind, fueling his rage to greater heights. Memories of his brother taking his last breath in his arms and of his mother crying over his casket at the funeral.

More peaceful memories surfaced. Ones of their childhood as identical twins. They would dress alike and play tricks on their teachers and girlfriends. His eyes welled up, but even through the tears he didn't and couldn't mistake the tall, lanky figure ahead of him, even amongst the females and dread-head Mafiosos. He eased the Glock 40 from under his shirt.

Swiftly, he maneuvered through pedestrians like a thief in the night. Huncho and the Mafia were so caught up in the moment they were completely unaware of his presence as he crept up on them. Ten feet away, Dre raised the Glock, and the ones closest to him began to scream and run.

Chapter 4

Camry was furious. She had been calling Huncho all night after receiving calls from a couple friends telling her he was hugged up with another girl at the game. She couldn't believe him. It was bad enough they were already having relationship issues due to other rumors of his unfaithfulness. They were just getting past the incident with a girl named Shea, who he supposedly had jumped by some Southside Queens.

She dialed his number for what felt like the 50th time only to get the same results. Voicemail. She cursed at her inability to leave a message due to it being full. "I'm so tired of his shit!"

She pulled up her recent call log and scrolled down to Yummy's name. She answered on the fourth ring, barely audible above the noise in the background. The music was blasting and her friends were laughing and yelling out of the window.

"Hello!" Her left hand was covering her right ear.

Camry pulled the phone from her face before bringing it back. "Bitch, stop yelling!"

"I can't hear you. Speak up!" Yummy told Tiara to turn the music down. "Now, what was you sayin'?"

"Sound like you at a party or something."

"Naw, we just leaving the game. Riverdale beat North Clayton. And, oh, them Grove Street hos jumped on Daja, girl. You should've seen 'em goin' at it out there. If it wouldn't have been for Southside Queens, Daja's ass would've been fucked up."

"So? I wish she would've." Bitterness laced Camry's tone. "I heard she sucked my man's dick in front of everybody just to be down with Southside Queens."

She couldn't have done nothin' he ain't let her, Yummy thought, but kept her feelings to herself. "Speaking of yo' man, I just saw him walking up the sidewalk, and he still with that girl. I think she go to Lovejoy."

"I ain't stuntin' his ass!" Camry lied, knowing Huncho was her reason for calling.

"Matta fact, there he go right there. I'm finna take his triflin'-ass the phone. Hold on." Yummy got out of the car in the middle of the gridlocked traffic, and jogged across the street with the phone pressed to her ear, giving Camry the 411 on everything she was seeing. She stopped in front of Huncho and the surrounding crowd. Shooting the girl he was with a nasty look, she held the phone out to Huncho. "Yo' baby mama want you!"

The thick, dark chocolate girl with honey-blonde highlights didn't respond or react to Yummy. She looked up at Huncho, who was smiling as if it was nothing to him. He removed his arm from around the girl, grabbed the phone, and put it to his ear as the crowd behind him began to scream and disperse. Thinking another girl fight had popped off, he turned to watch and found himself in the line of fire as Dre rushed toward him, barrel raised.

"Hit Squad Taliban, ho!" Dre yelled before pulling the trigger, letting off multiple shots.

The first slug hit Huncho in the neck, spinning him around as he fell to the pavement. The rest of the shots were fired into the scattering crowd of Queens and Mafiosos as they ducked for cover. The ones with guns began to bust back, but by the time they were able to do so, Dre had taken off on foot and blended in with the panic-struck crowd.

Yummy was squatting beside Huncho, screaming as she stared at the amount of blood gushing through his fingers as he held his neck. She had never seen so much blood in her life, and it was her first time actually seeing somebody get shot. She stood to her feet and began to scream for help. "Help! Somebody help me, please! He's dying!" she cried as she stared at her best friend's baby daddy. His eyes were wide and he looked to be choking, but she couldn't tell. She didn't like him because of the way he treated her friend, but she didn't want him to die. "Somebody!"

Camry heard the first gunshots, but Huncho dropped the phone and it broke once it hit the ground, disconnecting the call. She quickly dialed the number back, but got no answer. Fearing something was terribly wrong, she began to cry as she tried the number once more to no avail. She dialed another number.

A crowd began to gather around Huncho, one that was mostly Mafia. Flame had taken off his black T-shirt and pressed it against Huncho's neck as he knelt down beside him, Yummy standing to his right.

"Hold on, bra. Help on the way!" he said.

Bystanders, both male and female, who had love for Huncho stood around in disbelief, some sniffling and crying. The sound of more gunshots erupted, causing everyone to duck, but the shooting came from down the street where Mafiosos were shooting at suspected H.S.T. members.

As darkness overcame Huncho, he had one final thought: *I'm dying.*

Dre escaped without wound or capture. He'd run into the cover of the crowd and hightailed it up the street where Tevo, Marko, and Gotti awaited. Hopping in the car, they mashed out back to The Grove.

The Squad was posted twelve deep on Gotti's porch, barely visible. The porch light was off, and they had long since busted the streetlights that lined the cul-de-sac. Everyone was trying to figure out if Huncho was dead or not and who all had been shot. Their phones had been ringing constantly all night, but they acted as if they knew nothing about the incident. Let them tell it, they were never there.

Tevo hit the blunt, holding the smoke in his lungs. Passing the blunt to Dre, he exhaled. "You think that nigga made it, bra?"

"I don't know, shawdy." Dre shook his head, declining the blunt, and Tevo passed it to Kay-Nay. "I dome-called him and he dropped, but I had to jet 'cause some of them niggas was strapped. I hope that pussy-nigga dead. That's on my brother, shawdy!"

Tevo nodded. He felt his homeboy.

Gotti and Kebo came out of the front door as bright headlights from an approaching car illuminated the porch. They stood and began pulling straps from their waists, raising their hands to shield their eyes from the blinding light. The door opened and in the frame stood Cap, eyes narrowed, toting an AK-47 with a blunt hanging loosely from his lips.

The car stopped and Tevo's phone rang. He answered. "Yo? Oh shit, a'ight. Pull up. You good." He hung up and tucked his .45 back on his waistline. "Everything good."

Everybody went back to chillin' as the car pulled curbside in front of the house. Tevo's phone rang again. He answered, told the caller to get out and meet him halfway, then hung up. Tapping Dre, he motioned for him to follow, and they walked to the middle of the front yard.

Three females got out of the car, two from the front and one from the back. Brandi walked around the front of the car from the driver's side, the other two females following her lead. She reached Tevo, gave him a hug, and introduced him to the female who had exited the passenger's seat.

"This Shea." Brandi tilted her head, using the middle finger of her right hand to wisp her braids behind her ear. "She's the one I been tellin' you 'bout. The one Huncho had them girls jump."

Tevo noticed her instantly. "You just went in for The Grove at Tara Stadium, ain't it?"

Shea was taken aback by his recognition. She looked at Brandi, then back to Tevo and nodded. "Yeah, I mean, it was my beef. The Grove rode for me."

Tevo looked back at Dre, who offered a curt nod. He turned back to Shea. "A'ight, so everything green, then. Long as you ridin' for the cause, you good out here, shawdy. Ya ain't gotta worry 'bout shit, ya hear me?"

"I hear you," Shea nodded, relaxing a little. Behind her, Meka's phone went off. She answered, heading to the car so as not to disturb the conversation.

"Bet," Tevo said. "So, you know these niggas?"

"Yeah, something like that." Unable to hold his gaze, Shea glanced off, afraid her eyes would betray her.

As Tevo asked her if she knew where the Mafia be at, she thought of how by catching feelings for Huncho, she had ruined Brandi's plan to get in good with some frontline Mafiosos. As a result she, Brandi, Meka, and Zaria had gotten ran through for no reason, a fact no one outside of them knew. The setup was to be a surprise for Tevo. Mission failed, it would remain a secret.

In the meantime, they were friends and would have each other's backs. Shea wasn't from The Grove, nor did she claim to be, but living closer to the Riverdale Road side of Garden Walk, she could. In fact, a good number of people in her neighborhood did, especially the ones who repped the Squad. Previously she'd stayed out of the whole beef thing, but she felt bad for messing up Brandi's plan. Even when she did, Brandi didn't get mad and cut her off. She stood up for her. Whatever Brandi was with, she was with it, so to plug her in with Hit Squad's elite, Brandi was letting her reveal a location that was sure to get her some A-1 brownie points.

"He took me to this house they call The Spot off 138. It's on Lyle Drive"

Dre spoke up for the first time. "You remember where it's at?"

She nodded.

***

Huncho was lying in a hospital bed at Southern Regional wearing a neck brace, eyes trained on the wall-mounted television as the sun shone through the sheer white curtains draping the window. Fresh from a morphine-induced sleep, he was trying to figure out how long he'd been in the hospital. Three days felt like three weeks with all the sleeping he'd been doing. At some point he just lost count.

The last conscious memory he could recall was the doctor telling his mother and Camry the bullet went straight through with no major damage to his throat. At least he thought that was his last conscious memory. Seeing his mother, he wasn't exactly sure. He was surprised to see she remembered she had a son. He half believed he dreamed it, but it was whatever. Nothing had changed.

However, he was sure how he ended up in the hospital. His memory hadn't been impaired. He remembered exactly what happened. Most memorable was the look in the eyes of the shooter. It was like looking at the ghost of the guy he had killed. He could remember the fire spitting from the barrel right before he felt the hot lead tear into his neck. It was more of a burning sensation than pain when he first got shot. The pain came later, and it was intense. Huncho hoped he would never get shot again.

The doctor said the crook in his neck from being on the phone saved his life. All he could do was thank God and his angels for protecting him.

The door to the room opened, and he cut his eyes to see who was entering, but realized it was the nurse when he heard the cart rolling in. Clad in white scrubs, she strolled in behind the cart, skin a Caribbean sun-kissed brown. Her long dreads were stylishly wrapped and her assets were well proportioned.

"Oh, so you finally woke up, I see." She had a Jamaican accent. "How're you feelin'?"

With a slight nod of his head, he indicated he was alright. Fixing him a cup of water, she stuck a straw in it and put it to his lips. He closed his eyes as the water quenched his thirst. He hadn't realized before how bad his cottonmouth had been.

"Take your time now," she said. "Does it hurt when you swallow?"

He shook his head slightly, taking great care to exude just enough strength.

"Okay then. I gotta check your vitals, then I can let your visitors in." The nurse got Huncho squared away, then left the room, ass jiggling with each step she took.

Huncho wondered who had come to see him. He remembered seeing his mother and baby mama at his bedside before dozing off, and before that a couple Mafiosos and Queens had come through to check on him. He figured it was probably some more of them.

The door opened at last, and to his surprise two detectives entered, both wearing button-downs and slacks with their exposed badges clipped to their waists. He remembered then they had visited him as well. They questioned him about who had shot him, but he had no intention of cooperating at all. He could handle his own like the certified street nigga he was bred to be. The one he was.

The young white detective posted up by the door while the middle-aged black detective approached his bedside.

"Mr. Blanding, I'm Detective Ellis, and this is my partner, Detective Foster. We would like to ask you some questions about what happened to you," he said. "We were here yesterday, but you had just taken your medication. You feeling any better now?"

Huncho gave a stiff nod.

Ellis got right to the point. "Do you know who shot you?"

Huncho shook his head a little too quickly, and the detectives knew he was lying. Ellis looked back at Foster, then turned back to Huncho. "Do you have any idea why someone would want to shoot you? Because it seems like they were trying to take you out."

Kick rocks, detective. You're wasting your time, Huncho thought, shaking his head.

The detectives continued to question him, changing up strategies and sometimes tag-teaming him, hoping to get him to cooperate, but none of what they said meant anything to him. They came out better talking to each other until they asked him about his affiliation with the Mafia. That caught him off guard. If they hadn't had his full attention, they had it now.

"No, seriously, don't they call you Huncho?"

Detective Foster stared at Huncho, who stared back, unresponsive.

"Do you know a Deontae Chambers, A.K.A. Taliban?"

Huncho was growing uncomfortable with the line of questioning. He shook his head.

"Ever heard of Hit Squad Taliban?"

Huncho smirked, shaking his head once again.

"Okay then, smartass, I'ma tell you what I know," Ellis exploded, having grown tired of Huncho's games. "I know you run with Southside Mafia, and I know you killed Taliban for jumping on your boy Nard at Sparkles. Now, if you don't cooperate with me, I'll push this motherfucking bed to 9157 Tara Boulevard myself! You know where that is?"

Huncho shook his head, feigning ignorance.

"Well, that's the Clayton County Jail, asshole," Ellis spit. "I'll go get a murder warrant on your ass so fast it'll make your head spin! So, do you want to cooperate or not?

46

Because either way, you're going down. If I was you, I'd stay on my good side so I can help you when this shit hits the fan, 'cause your boys are talking. Your call. Deal or no deal?"

Huncho's face turned to stone as he looked the detective in his eyes and, for the first time since being shot, he spoke. "I didn't fall down from heaven," he said in a low, dry voice. "I came up from hell. Understand me, Detective-Whatever-Your-Name-Is? And before I betray the life I live, I'd rather die or spend the rest of my life in prison."

The seriousness in which he made the statement left the detectives both astonished and dumbfounded. They felt chills shoot through their bodies at the change in his demeanor. It was clear they were dealing with a real goon, one who was one thou-wow to what he believed in.

They looked at each other with uncertainty until Ellis found his voice again. "We'll be back to talk to you, so don't think you've gotten away, Huncho!" Then he left with Foster in tow.

Just as they were walking out, Camry and Yummy were coming in with balloons in their hands. Huncho faked a smile.

***

The Mafia had been combing the streets looking for the individual responsible for Huncho's attack. With no luck, they sent some females on an undercover mission to find the triggerman and his associates. Reka, a loyal member of Southside Queens, knew it would be easy to infiltrate the Squad due to her and Tevo's teenage love affair once upon a time ago. Rounding up Yana and Missy in her silver Kia, they shot to a spa on Old National Highway in College Park to get their hair, nails, and toes done. Then, in their best 'fits, they headed to The Grove.

47

Elijah R. Freeman

They'd been schooled by Flame on what to do, and as they rode, Reka went over the plan. Forever had passed since the last time she and Tevo communicated, and she doubted he knew of her affiliation with the Mafia. That being the case, her chances at success were good. After all, their breakup had been more over her moving away than anything.

Old National was a trip and a fall away from The Grove, and with a clear, sunny forecast ahead of them, Reka, Yana, and Missy were over-ready to put in work. Windows down, hair caught in the breeze, they whipped up on 4900 beating Crime Mob's *Stilettos*. They were crunk.

Cruising down Grove Street, Reka spotted four guys walking curbside by Aldi's. She got over and pulled alongside them. "Aye, y'all know Tevo?"

"Light-skin Tevo with the wavy hair?" one of them asked.

"Yeah, that's him," Reka smiled. "You know where I can find him?"

"Shid, he over on Crystal Lake. Just ride down through there," he said, pointing up the street toward the Quick Trip. "You'll see him out there."

"Alright, thanks." She pulled off, smiling.

Turning onto Crystal Lake Drive, she saw a group of people standing in a yard up the street, behind which sat a tan and white house. If she was lost, the green let her know she was getting warmer. She turned the music down.

"Y'all ready?" she said.

Yana rolled her eyes. "Girl, please."

Missy cut the music back up, and they laughed until they reached the thug-clustered yard.

On the porch, Tevo stood at the head of the small steps, hand tucked in his waistline, clutching his .45. Around him, others gripped various calibers of arsenal as well.

Triggadale

Reka turned into the driveway. All eyes were on the little Kia as it pulled in. Seeing it was full of females, they loosened up and moved in for a better view.

Reka cut the engine and stepped out of the car. Locking eyes with Tevo, she smiled. Surprisingly, he smiled back.

Damn. She had to admit he was looking good, but she shook it off. She was on a mission for the Mafia. Clouded judgment built upon the physical alone was suicidal.

"Tell yo' friends they can get out, too." Kebo took a swig from a 211 black can.

Reka looked back at Yana and Missy. "Might as well. Come on, let's chill for a minute."

They got out of the car and she turned around to find Tevo had made his way down the steps and was now only a few feet away. "What's up, stranger? Long time, no see."

"Yeah, it has been a while. Come here, let me get a hug." He spread his arms wide and she stepped into his embrace. "What brings you this way?"

"You. I ran across some of our old pictures while moving, and since you haven't tried to contact me in the last five years, I decided to find you."

Tevo released her from his embrace and stepped back to take her in from head to toe. She wore a pair of tight, faded jean capris with cocaine-white Air Force Ones and a short, black, curve-hugging shirt that left her lower torso exposed, revealing a cute navel ring. He thought about the way he used to fuck her and eat her pussy. She was the first girl he ever ate out, and from the way she was looking, he wanted another taste of the pie.

"It ain't like that, shawdy. I still think about you. We just lost contact." He shrugged. "Then, with you moving to the country and all –"

"Henry County is not the country!" Reka interrupted mid-sentence, attitude on a million. "And besides, I don't stay out there no more."

"Oh yeah? Where 'bout you stay now?"

"Out in Lovejoy, but I'm about to get my own place soon 'cause me and my step-dad just don't get along," she lied.

"So you came to find me so I can move in with you, huh?"

"Uh," Reka punched him in the arm playfully. "No!"

They laughed. Talked. Reminisced, even.

Hours later, Reka was surprised at the realization of how much history they shared. The secrets. The tears. The inside jokes. It was hard to forget someone who gave you so much to remember. The more they talked, the more Reka got caught up in the conversation, losing sight of what she was supposed to be doing. Liquor flowed, blunts burned, and of course, advances were made.

Yana and Missy seemed to be enjoying themselves as well, and although Missy was the least favored of the two, she held her own. Pretty or not, no one could argue her status as an asset. Yana, however, was on Kebo like red on High-Tec. The respect he got from his hood turned her on. All bullshit aside, fucking was definitely something he desired, but that was where the road capped off. He was far from a sucker.

Time soared, and by six that afternoon Reka and Tevo found themselves in her car, chillin', old feeling resurfaced.

"Tevo, I can't even lie." She took his hand in hers, locking fingers. "I missed you like crazy, boy."

"I missed you, too, shawdy."

Reka's phone went off. "Excuse me."

As she read, Tevo took note of her abrupt change in vibe, but chose to remain silent as she texted back, figuring from her reaction it was probably her boyfriend.

The message brought her back to the reality of what she was supposed to be doing, bringing with it an overwhelming feeling of guilt. Flame wanted to know if she'd found Tevo. She texted back that she was with him now and slid her phone in her left pocket.

50

Triggadale

"Who was that?" Tevo wore a crooked smile. "Your boyfriend checkin' up on you?"

"I told you I don't have a boyfriend, Tevo!" She made a face. "I have a friend."

He laughed. "Right, right, a'ight. Cool."

"And since you asked, yes, that was him. I have to go pick him up for work."

"Oh, so you got you a square, huh?"

Reka sucked her teeth. "Whatever. So, what you gonna be doin' later on? I want to come back and see you." She eyed him up and down. "Alone."

"Shid," Tevo shrugged nonchalantly. "You can do that. I'm chillin'. What time you talkin' 'bout?"

They arranged to link back up between nine-thirty to ten that night, then said their farewells.

On the way back to The Spot, Reka had mixed emotions about what she was about to do. Yana and Missy joked and laughed, too high to notice her thoughts were occupied.

By time they were pulling up on Lyle Drive, she was an emotional train wreck. She was unsure if she could go through with the plan. Tevo was her first love.

Elijah R. Freeman

Chapter 5

Dre turned off S.R. 138 onto Lyle Drive, following the directions Shea gave from the passenger seat. They rode up the street at a slow creep.

"Right there." Shea pointed to the house labeled The Spot by the Mafia. Two cars were in the driveway, one of them a silver Kia. It had just left The Grove, unbeknownst to Dre.

They continued on up the street, busted a "U", and swerved back. As Dre passed the house for the second time, he nodded. News of Huncho's survival had reached him, and he wasn't happy at all. Word on the curb was he'd been released from the hospital the day before. He was looking forward to finishing what he started.

"You sho that's the right house?" Lights were on inside and he could see movement through the curtains. Nothing out of the ordinary.

"Positive. That's the same silver Kia them hoes rode off in after they jumped me."

Again, Dre nodded, contemplating his next move. His heart bled for Huncho. Every breath he took was a spit on his brother's tombstone.

He chose his next words carefully. "Now, listen, you can't be runnin' yo' mouth when this shit go down." He stared ahead, eyes void of emotion, voice a chilly seriousness. "I mean to nobody, feel me?"

She cut her eyes his way. "I ain't gon' say shit." Shea didn't know why, but she felt the shift in his vibe. His threat was clear. Any sign of loose lips and it was a dundotta. She was game.

Just as the sun began to set, Dre dropped Shea off in Garden Walk Apartments. From there he headed to Crystal Lake Drive to holla at Tevo, Cap, Gotti, and Marko. He informed them of The Spot's location, and they pieced together a plot to strike. The time was set.

Midnight.

***

Huncho had come home a different person. It was like the gunshot had changed him. He was always aggressive, but now it was as if he was short-circuiting. Aside from Flame, everyone was subject to his rage. Mafiosos included.

More attentive of his surroundings, he was conscious of those around him at all times. Sitting behind him in any car, his or not, was a thing of the past. It was simple: he'd take the back or he wouldn't be riding.

One pistol was no longer sufficient. He toted two and wore a Teflon bulletproof vest. He was war-ready, not just for the opposition, but for the 'frienemies' as well. He spoke of cutting the eyes out of witnesses. Snatching up females from The Grove and fucking them with hot curling irons. Real Mafia shit!

"Fear works when respect won't do," he said.

His homeboys thought he was trippin', but there was nothing wrong with his mental. He was just being alert. Slipping was no longer plausible for him. During his hospital stay, Camry informed him she was having a girl. He was trying to be here for that.

That night at The Spot, Huncho was sitting in the living room on the long couch, a small bathroom trash can at his feet. On the edge of his seat, he sat hunched over the coffee table, on which lay two twin 9's, a small bankroll, and a few healthy buds of Gangsta Mid. He was breaking it down when Flame walked in and plopped down beside him.

"Say, bra, 'member the nigga I was tellin' you 'bout that be with ol' boy who shot you?"

Huncho removed a box of White Owls from his pocket, pulling one from the pack. "Yeah, what about him?"

Flame brought him up to speed about the setup, as he traced a line down the cigar with his tongue and held it over the small trash can, dumping the guts as he worked a split down the middle.

The sound of glass crashing to the floor came from the kitchen and Huncho paused, looking back. At the dining room table, Tee was re-twisting Tall-Teezzee's dreads, laughing at whatever had just happened.

"Fuck!" someone yelled.

Flame turned around. "Fuck was dat?"

"Slap stupid ass," Tall-Teezzee said.

No sooner had the words left his mouth when Slap-Rocks stormed out of the kitchen, headed to the hallway. "Jayvo!"

A voice called from the back room, "Yo!"

"Man, ain't no muthafuckin' dope in there, lyin'-ass nigga!"

Everyone in the backroom busted out laughing. Slap-Rocks went in, closing the door behind him.

Huncho turned back around and began breaking down buds. "What about the muthafucka that shot me? Ain't nobody locked in on him, yet?"

"That's what I'm tryna tell you. Man, ya boy don't play the radio. If it ain't family business, Squad affairs, or 'bout some paper, shawdy ain't fuckin' 'round. From what I hear, he's the quiet twin. Taliban was the wild one. Tevo can be used to get to him, though. He's Dre's right-hand, from what I hear."

Flame explained in depth, and before long Ski and Nard walked through the front door. Nard toted a black trash bag full of weed over his shoulder while Ski networked from his Metro, already setting up plays. Placing it on the dining room table, they went back out. Moments later they

Elijah R. Freeman

returned with an 84-inch plasma screen television, swapping it with the one in the living room.

Television set up, they busted the weed down, splitting it four ways. That's how the Mafia rolled. They didn't eat, they feasted together like *La Cosa Nostra*.

The sun set and Flame hit Reka to set the night's events in motion. He sensed a change in her attitude, but disregarded it when she said she was about to call him and head over to pick him up. An hour later she texted back, en route, Tevo riding shotgun.

Pulling up to the bando, she put her car in park, and cut the engine. Out the car and up the driveway, Tevo followed close behind. She had him fooled. To his understanding, the house ahead was hers, but that was the farthest thing from the truth. Reka had worked her one. Not that he was dumb. It was dark, and anybody could've gotten hit with it.

Reka fished through her purse, fake-looking for her keys. A few feet from the door, she accidentally-on-purpose dropped her purse. Squatting, she began recollecting the contents of her bag. Beside her, Tevo squatted, picking up the things that had fallen as well, using the light from his phone to see.

"Wrong side of town, muthafucka!" Flame jumped from the shadows in all-black, cracking Tevo across the face with the .9, splitting him above his brow.

Reka ran back up the driveway to her car and smashed out, swerving a hard left onto Mundy's Mill Road

"Ooh, shit, what the fuck!" He held his eye, trying to see as blood gushed through his fingers.

Ski and Nard emerged from the shadows, squaring off with him. Guard up, Tevo stood strong, ready for whatever. Ski swung a right, but Tevo side-stepped left, dropping him with a right hook. Nard and Flame rushed him and he stood in the paint, taking and giving licks all the same.

Ski ran back up and caught Tevo off guard with a power slug, sending him headlong to the ground. He caught

56

himself and got right, bouncing on his toes as he sized up his opponents. Guard up, he squared off once again.

Flame ran up, throwing heavy blows. Tevo tried to block, but caught one square to the jaw. He ducked one from Nard, landing an uppercut that sent him flying back into Ski just as Flame speared him to the ground, falling on top of him. Tussling, they wrestled for control, until Nard kicked Tevo in the face. He toppled over, face a bloody mess.

"Fuck that!" Flame yelled. "Nard, grab his arms!"

Nard grabbed Tevo's arms and Flame stomped him in his face, sending the back of his head smashing into the dirt. Dazed and defenseless, they pounced on him, punching, kicking, and stomping him until he was thoroughly fucked over. Flame stopped, pushed Nard back, and grabbed Ski by the shoulder, pulling him off Tevo. Dead men couldn't talk.

Standing over him, chests heaving, they struggled to catch their breath. The blow from the gun and kick to the head had Tevo disoriented. He lay stretched out, moaning and groaning as he held his midsection, willing the pain away. Covered in blood, he looked like a newly-initiated gang member. His nose and lip were busted, eyes and jaw swollen, body bloody, scrapes and cuts about his arms, legs, and face.

Grabbing his arms, they dragged him into the bando, leaving a trail of blood. The trail was from the front yard to the backside kitchen, a room lit with candles that couldn't be seen from the street. They let his arms go and he dropped to the floor with a thud. Huncho looked on in silence, dancing candle flames casting an ominous glow against his dreads, shrouding his face in darkness. He twisted the end of one, as they hung freely, a shining machete in his other hand.

Lifting a candle from the counter, he stepped over to Tevo, who was coming back to his senses. Huncho stared

57

down, dreads hanging low, machete and candle in hand. One glance at the looming figure and Tevo's eyes widened in shock. He tried to slide away, but was met by the barrel of an AK-47. He took in the four dark figures before him. All black everything: tees, gloves, jeans, shoes, guns. Behind them, their shadows stretched floor-to-wall. Taking in their dreads, it became clear who they were.

The muthafuckin' Mafia! Tevo thought. *Reka? She set me up. That bitch set me up!*

"Yo' boy, Dre. Where he at?" Huncho held the machete face level, eyeing it so as to ensure it was sharp. "I ain't fucked up 'bout murkin' yo' ass, shawdy."

"I don't e'en know what you talkin' 'bout, bra." Tevo spit a mouthful of blood. "Fuck!"

"Oh naw? So I guess yo' name ain't Tevo and you ain't from The Grove, either, huh?" Huncho said. "Don't worry, this should help you remember."

Huncho raised the machete and brought it down hard on Tevo's wrist, severing it from his forearm. Stuck in the wood floor, Huncho wiggled the blade back and forth to free it.

Tevo looked at his hand and screamed in agony as the pain and realization of what happened shot through his body. Flame, Ski, and Nard stared at Huncho in disbelief.

Maintaining his calm, he circled Tevo. "You know who I'm talkin' 'bout now, fuck-nigga?" Huncho pointed the machete at him. "Where the fuck the nigga at?"

Tevo had no intention of selling Dre out. He was loyal to Dre, and even more so to the Squad he claimed. Besides, he was going to die, and he knew it. Having lived the life of a gangsta, he was prepared to die the death of one.

Grimacing, he managed a chuckle. He looked from his amputated hand to Huncho's looming presence. "Probably with ya mama, pussy." He spit on Huncho's shoes. "Fuck you! Hit Squad Taliban for life!"

"What life?"

Huncho swung the machete at a horizontal angle, decapitating Tevo's head from his neck. His body fell sideways and his head rolled across the floor. He stuck the machete into Tevo's chest, leaving it there.

Ski threw up as Nard and Flame looked on in shock. Huncho dropped the candle to the floor and stared into the growing flames as they began to catch.

"Everything Mafia," he said.

Then he walked out the door.

***

Dre had been calling Tevo's phone for the last couple of hours. Midnight was at hand, and he was ready to ride out. He had unfinished business to attend to and was trying to handle it. From what Marko told him, some thick, dark-skinned female swung through earlier and scooped him up. But he knew Tevo. He'd never put a bitch before him or Squad business. Without a doubt, something was wrong.

He tried his number again and it continued to ring until the voicemail picked up. Full from his previous messages, he disconnected, sending him another text.

If he was fuckin' the bitch he was with, he would've turned his phone off, he thought. *Maybe the nigga locked up. Or shid, maybe he lost his phone or something.*

He called other Squad affiliates to see if they'd seen or heard from him, but it was the same with each number he called. Getting in his car, he stopped by Tevo's mother's house to learn he hadn't been home all day. Finally he called Shea and had her check with Brandi, but it was the same story.

With each call, his worries increased. Something wasn't right. It was unlike Tevo to pull a stunt like this. They always knew each other's whereabouts.

By 3:30 in the morning he decided to wait on hitting the house. Besides, his mind was somewhere else. He had to find Tevo. He couldn't put his finger on it, but something was telling him Tevo was in some type of trouble.

Chapter 6

A black and gold tour bus pulled up in front of Riverdale Park where the community was celebrating Clay County Day. It was a sunny afternoon and traffic was bumper-to-bumper as people mingled up and down Church Street by the thousands. The ones closest to the street strained to see who would step off the bus. They knew several rappers would be present, but when the door opened, a mob of guys in all black spilled out like blood from a slit wrist.

Shaking their tip-dyed dreads side-to-side, the crowd recognized who they were at once and parted like the Red Sea to let them through. Some bounced forward screaming "M-A-F-I-A," while others simply threw up the *M*s.

Benji Gang was on the makeshift stage, their label's performing artist dead center. Purp, the founder, was also center stage. Tall and brown, he sported waist-length dreads with purple highlights that he wore in two big braids going back along the left and right sides of his head, his stylishly-wrapped hang time dropping mid-back.

He and Huncho met last summer in the County as bunkmates. It was Huncho's first time. Purp liked how he moved, Huncho fucked with his drip, and before long a mutual respect was formed between the two. They had been rocking ever since, mostly on the work tip. Seeing Huncho, he gave the Mafia a shoutout.

Halfway to the stage, Fat Mike stole on a random guy whose only offense was being too close to a live wire. The Mafia took off on him, swinging relentlessly. Beating him to the ground, they stomped him out. The Mafia had shown up a hundred deep, so trying to stop them from doing them was impossible.

Their first victim for the day had them hyped, but the beat-down increased police presence. The ambulance arrived shortly thereafter, and EMT personnel hauled the

Elijah R. Freeman

victim off on a stretcher to an awaiting ambulance. The crowd settled and five Mafiosos were called to the stage to perform their hit song and official anthem, *Yep! Southside Mafia.*

Followed on stage by thirty other Mafiosos, it wasn't hard to get the audience to catch the vibe. A local hit, the crowd rapped along as the performance began. Everyone was hyped except for one group of people standing off to the side, mugging.

Hit Squad Taliban.

They were thick in Riverdale Park as well. Dre stared at Huncho, who stood amongst his crew like a Big Dog. Knowing a shootout could land them in a cell, he and Huncho let the beef sizzle for another day, staring each other down with pure hatred in their eyes.

Flame leaned into Huncho. "That's ya boy, ain't it? Wanna do his ass, now?"

"Naw, let the bitch-nigga live to hear about what I did to his partna."

Flame joined the stare-down. Forming a pistol, Huncho raised his hand, aimed it at Dre, and pulled the trigger.

Dre nodded, mouthing, *I'ma get you first.* Then he turned, directing his crew through the crowd, Huncho watching until they were out of sight.

Finished performing, they loaded back onto the tour bus, into the cars that followed with some females they picked up along the way. Inside the bus, the party continued as they crept through the slow-moving traffic down Church Street. Huncho and Flame were in the back of the bus with a few Queens. They weren't into the females who sat rolling up blunts as they pleased. They were more in tune to the conversation they were holding amongst themselves.

"Man, we should've flipped them niggas while we had the chance, bra."

62

"For what? So a nigga could tell on us?" Huncho shook his head. "We ain't goin' out like that. Another time and place will present itself. Just be patient. In the meantime, let's enjoy this day."

Flame nodded, digesting his homeboy's wisdom.

A bottle of Patron was passed back, and just like that, they were riding a different vibe. One of the females they picked up decided to show her dancing skills and started stripping. The Mafia showered her with money, and it led to a couple of other girls taking their clothes off to dance as well. Later that night, they pulled up at the Ritz and went in the club fifty-deep.

***

Ms. Jackie sat in front of her television, crying with a picture of her son in one hand and a wad of tissue in the other. The eleven o'clock news was on, and family members sat around her with their eyes trained on the television screen, not believing what happened. As the coverage ended and went to another story Ms. Jackie broke down.

"Oh Lord, why you take my baby from me?" She slid off the sofa to the floor, shaking her head as she sobbed. "My baby ain't hurt nobody. Why they do him like that?"

Tevo's scorched corpse had been identified through dental records after being found amongst the debris of a torched house. The gruesome discovery was the top story on every local news channel in Atlanta and all its surrounding counties. When his mother was notified, she didn't believe it and thought it was some kind of joke until she was presented with the facts. When she found out he had been decapitated, she passed out.

"They didn't have to do my baby like that," she sobbed over and over.

"It's gonna be alright. The good Lord don't make no mistakes, chil'. Your baby is in a better place now." Her elderly neighbor spoke in a soft, soothing, motherly tone, rubbing her back in a consoling manner. "Probably looking down on us right now. I'm sure he wouldn't be much happy to see you carrying on in such a way. Get yourself together. We're all praying for you."

Ms. Jackie wasn't the only one taking the news hard, though. A friend of Brandi's who knew she messed around with Tevo texted her the police report. She called back to confirm the news.

"It was on the news. I saw it myself," Brandi's friend from Cedar Creek said. "Plus his mama stay down the street from me, and it's a lot of cars over there."

"Please tell me you lyin', girl. I know my baby ain't dead!" Brandi was distraught.

"I wouldn't even play with you like that, B. They say they found him inside a burned down house with his head cut off."

Brandi screamed, dropping her phone. Zaria picked it up, asked what was going on and got informed of the news.

Brandi got herself together and called Dre. He was at the club when he received the news and ended the call without so much as a word.

"What's up with you, bra?" Marko could tell by Dre's facial expression that something was wrong. They stood with Hit Squad Taliban off to the side in J-Paul's, watching the crowd. "You a'ight?"

Dre was barely audible over the loud music. "Tevo dead, shawdy. They found his body in a burned down house off Mundy's Mill on Fitzgerald."

"Naw, man! Naw! Not Tevo, shawdy." Marko's face twisted in anger and disbelief. "I just holla'ed at him a few days ago. What the fuck!"

Back-to-back everyone's phone went off as calls and text messages poured in about Tevo. He had been one of the top dawgs, a *Corleone*, and a solid nigga to back the title. Losing him was a huge loss for the Squad. Some poured out beer and liquor inside the club, while others shed tears openly, but it all came to an abrupt end when Southside Mafia was spotted entering the club.

"Aye, Dre, the door." A Squad affiliate named Meat Man nodded his head toward the entrance. "Look who just came in."

At the sight of Southside Mafia, Dre's mind flipped. He stormed through the crowd. Crew on his heels, he took one final swig from his Corona bottle. Dre was no fool. Tevo's murder was too gruesome not to be personal. It was no regular slaying. It was a message. He wanted the Mafia off the map. While he breathed the breath of the living world, he silently vowed to see to their demise. Personally.

It was probably a good thing he wasn't strapped right then, because with the way he was feeling, he would've dome-called as many Mafiosos as his clip allowed right there in front of the club. He had zero understanding.

Pushing and shoving his way through the crowd, he got a better view of his enemies. Frontline was Huncho. Dre saw red.

Huncho put his phone on vibrate, looking up just as Dre was coming down with a Corona bottle. Huncho weaved the blow, triggering a sharp pain in his neck from the sudden movement. He punched Dre in the jaw, knocking him sideways. The Squad and the Mafia were now throwing hands, and the club lights came on as the two crews went at each other.

Dre caught his balance and went at Huncho with all he had. The two stood, going blow-for-blow until Huncho's wounded neck slowed him down and one of Dre's blows caught him square in the chin, knocking him to the floor.

Just as Dre went to stomp him out, Huncho pulled a custom .38 with a Glock barrel from his pants and fired at Dre, barely missing him. At the sound of gunfire, the club erupted in panic, stampeding toward the exit. He jumped to his feet, psyched from being knocked out, but Dre had already dipped and blended into the crowd.

Police stormed the club, and Huncho scanned the crowd for Katrina in a panic. She'd snuck the pistol in, but took flight at the sound of the gunfire, so he had no one to pass the gun off to. He didn't want to throw it away due to it being one-of-a-kind, so he stuck it back in his pants on his waistline and tried to blend in with the crowd.

On his way out of the club, he was snatched up at the door after being fingered by security as one of the fighters. A quick search and the pistol was found. He was taken to the Clayton County Detention Center for disorderly conduct, affray, possession of a firearm, and carrying a concealed weapon.

***

Reka sat in her bedroom crying her eyes out. Her mother knocked on the door several times throughout the day to see what the problem was, but got nowhere. She had been locked in the room all day, surfacing only to use the restroom. Her friends called the house and her cell, but she refused all calls. She didn't want to talk to or see anyone. All she wanted was to be alone in her room. No television. No radio. No visitors.

Word of Tevo's murder reached her early that morning when she woke up and checked her text messages. It was hard to fathom someone she knew and had just seen with his head decapitated, but when she watched the morning news and saw the patch of land where the house on Fitzgerald once stood, she began to cry and feel sick. To her knowledge they were only going to jump Tevo. Flame never said anything about killing him. Now Tevo was dead, blood was on her hands, and the scent was strong. Had she

66

known they were going to kill him, she wouldn't have set him up, and that was the bottom line.

In over her head, she now saw with 20/20 vision that this war between Southside Mafia and Hit Squad Taliban had escalated to an infamy similar to the west coast Crip and Blood beef. Not even two full months since Taliban's death, and already there was another casualty, not to mention Huncho's close call.

What had started out as fun, rapping, and simply putting on for their side of town had evolved into something fatally out of control.

Reka had known Huncho and Flame since middle school, but became close friends of theirs in ninth grade when they beat up her ex for pouring juice on her head in the cafeteria, all because she no longer wanted to talk to him. She asked what made them stand up for her, and they said he disrespected her in front of everyone, and they felt like that was some sucka shit.

She chalked it up as game, but they never tried her sexually in any way whatsoever. The years that followed only served to make them closer. They were like brothers, and she was the sister they never had. That was before the Mafia, the Squad, or any clique in Clayton County, for that matter, was even thought of. It felt like a lifetime ago now. She didn't even recognize Huncho and Flame anymore. Their status had turned them into heartless strangers. So much so she herself feared them, as well. She was scared to admit it, but she wanted out of the Mafia. Things had gone too far this time.

There was a knock at the door. "Sweetie, you okay in there?" It was her mother. "Some of your friends are here to see you."

Reka sat quietly, hoping to God her mother would go away if she remained silent. But when her mother demanded she open the door, she reluctantly got up and did just that. The moment her mother laid eyes on her usually gorgeous face, she knew something was terribly wrong. Her eyes and nose were red and swollen from crying, and her normally well kept up-do was disastrously disheveled.

Seeing the look on her mother's face, she broke down into heaving sobs. Her mother wrapped her arms around her, led her over to the bed, and consoled her grieving daughter with motherly love and understanding.

"Baby, what's wrong? Tell mama 'bout it." Her tone was soothing as she held Reka and rubbed her back. "It's alright. Just let it all out."

Her mother had recently learned of Tevo's death from Yana and Missy in the living room. They told her he was a schoolmate and had once been Reka's boyfriend, of course leaving out the fact they played a key role in his undoing.

Once they mentioned he was a old boyfriend from a past neighborhood Reka lived in, she knew exactly who they were talking about. Reka's biological father caught Tevo in her bed late one night. He moved them to Henry County, but the move only succeeded in making her rebel even harder until finally her father had enough. Feeling it was best her mother raise her, he sent her back to Riverdale.

She couldn't get back to Riverdale fast enough. Now she was wishing with all her heart she had behaved herself and stayed within the comfort of her father's predominantly white, suburban neighborhood.

Reka calmed down enough to tell her mother the cause of her emotional breakdown, minus her involvement in it. After some motherly love and reassurance, her mother headed downstairs to the living room to allow Yana and Missy to go up to Reka's room to see if they could bring her out of her present state.

"You alright?" Yana felt sorry for Reka, but more than anything she was glad she wasn't in her shoes.

"Yeah, I'm good." A fresh set of tears streamed down her face and she swiped them away.

Missy gave Reka a hug and offered her sympathy. She felt bad for Reka, but was a Queen to the fullest and felt Tevo's death was necessary. In fact, she had known the whole time Tevo would be killed. The Squad had disrespected the movement she vowed to support and defend until death at all cost. In her eyes the Squad's transgression was unforgivable, and what Dre did to Huncho warranted the utmost retribution.

Yana spoke first. "I thought they said they were just going to beat his ass?"

"That's what they told me," Reka sniveled, wiping away a tear.

It didn't sit well with Missy how nervous Reka's demeanor was or, worst of all, that she had yet to stop shedding tears for a major enemy of the Mafia. She wouldn't jump to conclusions, but she would watch for signs of treachery.

"You know Huncho got locked up at J-Paul's on Tara Boulevard last night?" Missy said to change the subject.

Reka looked surprised. "For what?"

"That lame-ass nigga Dre tried to sneak him with a bottle. Girl, we set that bitch off. Them Grove Street hos ain't talkin' 'bout shit. Me and Yana was whoopin', like, four of they ass by ourselves. You should've seen Alicia, though, girl. She got all her weave snatched out by some dyke bitch named Terri from The Grove." Yana was running her mouth a mile a minute. "I saw her in Kimberly Forest Apartments that time we pulled up on The Grove when D-Day was suppose to get a one with that nigga Trav Corleone they be worshipping. I ain't gonna lie, she can fight, but damn, Alicia need to step it up. Anyway, next thing I know Huncho pulls out a gun in the club and starts shooting. Everything got crazy after that. Next time we see Huncho, he gettin' patted down in handcuffs. When I saw the police grip his gun on his waistline, I already knew they were finna lock him up."

Everything Yana said was news to Reka. In the past she never needed an update because she was always on the scene. She missed last night's event due to her laying low. She had called herself dodging a possible run-in with Tevo. To think, it was all in vain. Not that she was disappointed about missing the action. It just still seemed unreal to her.

They continued to talk for an hour until they raised Reka's spirits enough to leave the house. They waited while she showered and dressed, and when she was ready, they hopped in the Kia and headed to Underground in downtown Atlanta.

Reka's phone started to ring as they hopped on the expressway. It was Flame. She sent his call straight to voicemail, having decided while showering that she would not associate herself with the Mafia. She knew it was easier said than done, but she was determined to give it up. If she couldn't do it safely cold turkey, she would try the slowly-but-surely route. She was serious, though. In her heart, she was through.

Right after she sent Flame to the voicemail, he texted Missy. He wanted to know if she had seen Reka.

Chapter 7

It was night out, and Huncho had just been released from the county jail after sitting for a week. The charges got dropped due to the officer not showing up at Huncho's first hearing, probably because he hadn't turned in the pistol he took from Huncho the night shit popped off with the Squad at J-Paul's. Seeing as it was a custom-made gun, he kept it for his personal gun collection and basically let Huncho walk free. Luck, some would say, but from what he'd experienced, he took it as a sign.

In the county he had seen Squad affiliates he'd never seen before. One he had stole on after peeping the H.S.T. tattoo with '4900' stamped on the right of the letters and '3700' to it's left.

The rest of his stay in the county he continued to hold it down, but he wasn't lost to the fact the Squad outnumbered the Mafia in almost every dorm. The Mafia had numbers, but nothing in comparison to the Squad. The stories he heard about how the Squad was doing the Mafiosos they caught down bad in certain parts of the detention facility made his blood boil, especially one he heard about a Mafioso who was jumped at church and lost a tooth.

What irked him was most of the ones claiming H.S.T. in the county had just recently been put down during their county bid. No matter where they got down, though, the Squad still had the ups behind the wall. Fortunately, he rode his time out without ending up on the short end of the stick.

Home again, the first thing he noticed was how much the Mafia had grown. Southside Mafia's headcount had literally doubled in a week's time. It was definitely a far cry from the county jail. It seemed liked everybody in Clayton County wanted in on the Mafia or was walking around rapping their songs. Some even wore "Free Huncho and B-

Smeezee" shirts. Huncho felt the love and all, but they could take the shirts off now.

He was back like he never left.

***

It was eleven o'clock at night, and instead of Huncho running the streets as he usually would, he was at The Spot in his room, laid up with Camry. They had been laying up day and night since he came home. Riverdale was hot. Known clique-poppers from both sides were being snatched up left and right regarding a shootout that took place at Riverdale Park. Tragically, it ended with the death of a five-year-old boy who got caught in the crossfire. The boy's older sister was shot as well, but her injuries weren't fatal. Just a bullet to the thigh. In and out.

Faces from both cliques where displayed on the news as wanted suspects, and so far eight of the Mafia's frontline hard-hitters had been arrested and tried on a variety of charges. The one charge they were all hit with was the Georgia Gang Act Law. They stayed solid and held it down, though. Nobody on either side snitched or relinquished any information, period.

"Huncho, why won't you just leave that gang stuff alone before you get killed or end up in prison?" Camry asked. "I want you to be here to help me raise our child, not in someone's jail or graveyard."

"Shawdy, why you e'en talkin' like that? You tryna jinx a nigga, ain't ya?" Huncho pinched her cheek playfully. "Besides, ain't nothin' gonna happen to me, girl."

"Huncho, please, you've already been shot and been to jail, and both times you got lucky. Don't you think God's trying to tell you something?"

He shrugged. "Probably so. Ain't no tellin'. But that's just part of the game, baby."

"Then you got everybody saying you killed that boy at Sparkle's. Did you do it?"

"Hell naw, shawdy!" Huncho snapped. "Where you getting yo' information, anyways? For real, like, straight up! Who feedin' you this bullshit?"

"Everybody I talk to be talking about how you killed that boy, and now they're saying you probably had something to do with that body they found in that burned down house. It's the talk of Riverdale."

Huncho looked at Camry and in his eyes was the glare many around him had bore witness to. Not Camry, though. Never before had she seen in him this coldness. It was an expression she had never beheld, and it made her second guess her opinion about the rumors floating about.

Is he actually capable of killing someone? she thought.

"Look, whoever the fuck you been talkin' to, you need to tell 'em to keep my muthafuckin' name out their mouth before they end up hurt, understand me?"

Camry recoiled to her side of the bed. "Daldrick, you're scaring me."

Huncho got up from the bed and began dressing. "Get dressed."

Reluctantly, she got up from the bed and began doing just that, the conversation they just had heavy on her mind. Huncho threw on a red-and-black Dickies suit with a matching pair of retro Jordan's and walked out, heading to the living room. He stood beside the long couch.

"Say, Ski," Huncho said.

Ski looked up from the coffee table. He and Shoota had pulled up some chairs so they could bag up some zips of weed. The table in the dining room was occupied due to a spade game. "Yo?"

"You be going to school still?"

"Hell yeah, why?"

"I need you to do some crowd control. Too many folks got my name in their mouth, and that ain't good."

Elijah R. Freeman

"A'ight, so what's up?"

"Nothing, really. Just come up with a fake name and let everybody know to spread a rumor 'bout him knocking ol' boy off."

"That's a bet."

"'Preciate ya, bra. It might not do too much, but I gotta start plantin' some doubt. That gossipin'-ass school got my baby mama catchin' wind of this shit."

Ski put his fist to his mouth, astonished. "No! Dead-ass?"

Huncho nodded, clearly frustrated as music began playing from the living room stereo. Flame had just popped in Young Jeezy's "Trap Or Die" mixtape.

"Damn," Ski said. "I'm saying, though. I mean, she trippin'?"

Huncho shook his head just as Camry stepped into the living room. "Naw, she good. I'm 'bout to dip, though. I'll be back later."

"A'ight." Ski gave him some dap.

Huncho headed to the door, Camry right behind him. He allowed her to go out before him, following after closing the door behind him. On their way to his car, a small van made an abrupt stop in the middle of the street.

Huncho was unlocking the driver's side when the van's side door slid open and someone with a green bandana tied around their face emerged with an AR-15 aimed from his waist. In the blink of an eye Huncho shifted to fourth gear, pulling two .40 calibers from his waist and opening fire, squeezing both triggers.

"Get in the car and lay down!" he yelled to Camry.

The guy with the AR-15 started shooting at the same time, followed by three other shooters with green bandanna-covered faces, leaving Huncho no choice but to dive in front of the car and duck. He could hear Camry screaming, and as crazy as it may sound, it comforted him. As long as he could hear her, he knew she was alive.

74

Crouched where he was, he could hear bullets whistling by, tearing into the side of the house and hitting the car he hid behind. Just as the shooters began to advance on The Spot, the front door flew open.

Ski came out guns blazing, but didn't make it far before he was met by a round from a Mac-11, knocking him off his feet. Other Mafiosos returned fire from inside the house, and the four shooters began to retreat to the van, diving in one-by-one.

Huncho came up firing both pistols sideways, running toward the van, then suddenly it took off. The gunman with the AR-15 was hanging out the window, still letting off shots as they fled the scene. Huncho made it to the street, still firing rounds into the back of the van until both guns were clicking, signaling his empty clips.

"Fuck!" He stood in the middle of the street, hammers on both pistols cocked back to display empty chambers.

"Daldrick!" Camry cried.

He hurried to his car, taking in the damage done to his Charger. It looked worse than the car that got flipped on Four Brothers. The windows was shattered, and every inch of the chassis was covered with bullet holes. The sight of it had him on edge as he began to imagine what he might discover inside.

Snatching open the passenger door, he pulled Camry into his arms, examining her. "Shh, you good now. Just calm down. You a'ight? You not hit anywhere, are you?"

Camry was so frantic he couldn't even understand her response, but from what he could see, outside of maybe a little trauma, she was alright.

"Ski got hit up, bra!" Flame yelled from the door, causing his attention to shift to the house, which now resembled a strainer.

Shoota and Tall-Teezzee came out gripping pistols just as Flame knelt down over Ski. Daja, Tee, and Missy came out next. Hearing movement, Huncho snapped to attention, but relaxed once he saw who it was. Nard, Jayvo, 8-Ball, and D-Day were coming from the side of the house. They had gone out the back door and came back around after the shooting stopped just in case a second van showed up or the one that just left doubled back. Up and down Lyle Drive, lights came on as the neighborhood woke up. A few people had even stepped out on their porches to see what was going on.

"Yeah, pull up," Nard said. He was talking to someone on the phone. "We down the street at The Spot. You ain't just hear all that shit!"

"Oh my God, no !" Tee screamed as she crumbled to the ground in tears. Missy squatted, trying to console her.

The sudden outburst drew Huncho's attention to the front of the house. Flame's hand was on Ski's neck in search of a pulse. When Flame shook his head, he already knew what it was. Shoota was slowly shaking his head as a tear slid down his face. He and Tall-Teezee were standing over Flame and Ski, looking down.

"Shit!" Huncho seethed, beginning to feel overwhelmed. He knew he had to focus, but it was hard to think straight with Camry crying hysterically in his ear.

He stood up as Nard approached, and Camry's cries got even louder. Jayvo, 8-Ball, and D-Day walked over to where Ski's bloodied, bullet-ridden body lay sprawled out in the yard.

"Who was that?" Huncho asked Nard.

Nard pointed down the street. "T.D. 'bout to pull up. Matta fact, there he go now."

Huncho turned to look just as T.D. pulled up in his money-green '85 Cutlass. He stopped in the middle of the street and hopped out, leaving his car running. A fine, dark-skinned woman was getting out on the passenger's side. Huncho only knew her as T.D.'s girl. They lived on Lyle Drive, as well, and had just come from down the street. As an original Mafia face, T.D. had come to clean house.

76

Huncho reached in his pockets for his keys as the faint sound of sirens approached. He had to get Camry away from there.

"Aye, here, bra." He handed them to Nard. "Look, take my car and duck it off in the back of Lake Ridge by the elementary school before them folks pull up. I'll go back for it later."

"Say no mo'!" Nard headed straight for the driver's side.

T.D. walked up as Nard was walking off. "What the fuck just happened?"

"Them fuck-ass Squad niggas, that's what!" Huncho pulled Camry to her feet. She was no longer hysterical, but her body was trembling as she continued to cry, trying to talk to Huncho at the same time. "Cam, please! I don't e'en know what you saying. I keep telling you, you good. Now chill out so I can think straight."

Huncho slammed the passenger door, 'causing the rear window to cave in. Camry jumped at the sound of the glass falling and began to cry harder as Nard started the car and backed out of the yard.

Huncho turned back to T.D. just as his girl reached his side. "Big bra, fuck with me on the whip for the night. I gotta get shawdy home. Flame got things here."

"Enough said." T.D. nodded. "Go 'head, take off."

"'Preciate ya," Huncho said.

He grabbed Camry and they headed to the running Cutlass in the middle of the street. Helping Camry in the passenger seat, he closed her door and hopped behind the wheel, slamming the driver's side door. Camry was still crying as he mashed out.

"See, I told you, Daldrick!" she sobbed. "I told you!"

"Would you shut the fuck up!" He fishtailed onto S.R. 138. Irate, he slammed his fist into the steering wheel, fuming. "I'ma kill them niggas!"

Elijah R. Freeman

Chapter 8

New Macedonia Baptist Church looked gloomy under the pale sky. The parking lot was filled with cars, making it look as though hundreds were attending the funeral. Tevo's outgoing personality and loyalty to his friends showed at the end of his life with the many faces that had come to say their final farewells. The sanctuary was so packed that many had to stand during the service.

Reka was one of them. She stood in the back, wishing she'd never come. The cold stares she received from Hit Squad Taliban had her nervous. Some even whispered to each other and glanced her way. She started to leave during the eulogy, but didn't want to show signs of guilt. That in mind, she remained until the end of the service, putting together a lie for anyone who questioned her about Tevo and the night she picked him up.

The ceremony ended and everyone filed out of the church exit, headed to the Roundtree Road Cemetery for the burial.

"Aye, shawdy!" Reka looked back as Marko approached, coming down the front steps of the church. "Reka, ain't it? You the one that scooped Tevo up that night from Gotti's."

Nervous and uncomfortable by the way he was mugging, her eyes welled with tears, lips quivering as she began talking. "Yeah, I picked him up. That was the last time I saw him." She began to cry. "We got into an argument and he told me to let him out the car. Said he'd catch the bus or find a ride home."

Marko eyed her suspiciously. "An argument, huh?"

"Yeah, he was upset because I answered my boyfriend's call while we were together. We had words and he told me to let him out the car, so I did," she lied. "Now I wish I wouldn't have, because if I hadn't, he'd still be here." She broke down crying and some heavy-set, brown-skinned lady came over and hugged her.

The tears she shed were real, but her story was fake. It didn't matter, anyway. Marko hadn't believed a word she said. None of it fit Tevo's character. He wasn't the type to argue with a female about anything, let alone another nigga. Even if that was the case, he would've called somebody from The Grove to pick him up. In fact, he would've called before he got out the car.

"Who li'l shawdy is, bra-bra?" Dre walked up as Tevo's female family member walked Reka to her car.

"That's the bitch Tevo left with the night he got murked." Marko eyed Reka with a glare of vengeance. "I don't believe shit she just said."

Before Dre could comment any further, Brandi, Meeka, and Zaria walked up. "What the fuck is that ho doing here?" Brandi snapped. "She one of the one's jumped on Shea!"

Dre's facial expression was now a look of bemusement as he thought about the day he and Shea rode past The Spot. The Kia that sat in front of the house that day was the same Kia Reka was getting in now.

"Say bra, is that the same car she picked Tevo up in?" Dre's eyes were locked in on Reka's car. It was too much of a coincidence that the female who picked Tevo up was driving the same car he had seen at The Spot only hours before he was killed.

"Yeah, that's it. What's up?"

That was all the confirmation he needed. "Follow her."

"Bet." Marko stepped away, raising his phone to his ear.

Brandi sucked her teeth. "Fuck all that 007 shit! We finna fuck this ho up now!"

"Naw, B." Dre grabbed her by the arm. "Revenge is best served cold. Let her ride out. She already dead, and she don't e'en know it."

80

Triggadale

***

With the two recent murders of Tevo and Ski, Detective Ellis and the special task force were forced to start picking up members from both sides of the war again. They could hold validated affiliates for up to 72 hours without charging them with anything, but they were sadly mistaken if they thought they would get a break in either of the cases. Both organizations stood firm and stuck to the G-Code of the streets.

"Come on now, Blanding, I know you know something. You're the man, I hear. Why don't you go ahead and tell me who killed your boy when they shot up your house, 'cause word is the bullet was meant for you." Ellis stopped pacing back and forth in front of Huncho and sat on the edge of the interrogation room table. "I know you were there that night. Your car was found in the back of Lake Ridge riddled with the same caliber bullets as the house on Lyle Drive. I'm not stupid. You shot it out and pulled off before the police got there, didn't you? Come on now, Blanding. Give up the goods on how you stood up for the Mafia that night."

Huncho sat slouched in the chair, twisting one of his dreads with a nonchalant look on his face. Ellis stared at him intently, the time he questioned him at the hospital fresh on his mind. He wasn't really expecting him to cooperate. He was more focused on catching him in a lie.

Huncho played his hand like a vet, though. Fuck a fold. He knew the game they were playing and knew not to speak. If they had anything on him, they wouldn't be asking questions. So he remained silent and continued twisting his hair.

Foster stormed into the room, slamming the door. "So, this is how you want to play it? Well, fuck it, we'll just go

Elijah R. Freeman

ahead and charge you with the murder and work the deal with your boy Howard, since he's willing to cooperate."

At the mention of Flame being a rat, Huncho smiled. "You know what? Y'all two muthafuckas could probably make more money as comedians, 'cause y'all funny as hell." He shook his head, releasing a chuckle. "Now, if y'all ain't got nothin' better to talk about, take me back to jail, 'cause I'm tired of hearing this bullshit."

Losing it, Detective Ellis hopped off the end of the table and grabbed Huncho by the collar, snatching him up from the chair he was sitting in and pinning him to the wall. Huncho showed no resistance, letting the detective have his way. Ellis' face was so close he could smell his breath and feel the heat of it when he spoke.

"You look here, you little twerp. You might be the shit in the street and with your little gang flunkies, but I run this muthafuckin' shit in here! You got that?" Ellis said through clenched teeth. "And before it's over with, I will have your ass off the street. That's if somebody doesn't kill you first."

Detective Foster placed his hand on Ellis' shoulder, causing him to cut his eyes at the hand that remained. "He's not worth it, Ellis. He'll slip sooner or later. Let him go."

Ellis gave him one final jerk before releasing his vise-like grip on Huncho's shirt. Huncho stared him down, muggin'. Foster stepped in, easing the tension by steering Ellis toward the door. Both walked out, closing the door behind them, and for the next couple of hours Huncho was left to his thoughts until a deputy showed up to return him to the jail.

Ellis and Foster tried the same tactic on other Mafiosos as well as Hit Squad Taliban members, but they all held firm, keeping their business in the street and staying solid. Three days later, those who hadn't been charged with a crime were released. The ones who weren't had probation holds or violations.

82

Triggadale

Huncho, Flame, and other Mafiosos that were released made it home in time for Ski's funeral, which was held under a clear autumn sky. Undercovers attended the funeral as well, following them to the cemetery, taking pictures from their cars. Some Mafiosos gave them the finger to let them know the Mafia was aware of their presence. Cover blown, there was no reason to hide. They got out and stood besides their cars with their cameras in hand. Ski's parents and family were surprised at the officers and felt disrespected by their presence.

After the burial was complete and everyone was leaving the gravesite, Huncho and Flame hopped off in Flame's Mustang and drove past the undercovers, shooting birds as they rode by. Flame was driving.

"We might have to lay low for a while. These bitches is on our ass!" Flame checked his rearview. "Shit, here they come, now. Watch this, I hope they got something under that hood!" Flame smiled, mashing the gas and causing the Mustang to lunge forward.

The undercovers' car was just completing a U-turn to follow them, but quickly learned they would have to try again another day.

***

It had been weeks since Tevo's funeral, and everything had been quiet between the two crews. Some saw each other in traffic, but remained calm due to the investigation. Many had been barred from certain clubs for fighting or shooting.

The only ones who were still active in the streets were the females. Reka fell back for a week or two, thinking of different excuses whenever her fellow Queens would question her unusual absences, but lately she'd been hanging with Southside Queens on occasion. Huncho and

Elijah R. Freeman

Flame were another story. She stayed away from them as much as possible.

She still felt bad about Tevo and the part she played in his murder. So bad she'd been having nightmares, waking up sweating and out of breath. They were always the same. She'd pull up at an abandoned house in a wooded area. Getting out of the car, she would walk up to the door and open it, finding Tevo's headless body. The head would be nowhere in sight, but she would hear him calling her name. She would run to the car, and once she got in, the head would be in the passenger seat staring at her. It got to the point she slept with her light on and wouldn't drive her car alone at night.

She was out alone today, getting her nails done at a shop in a plaza off S.R. 138, when Daja called. She answered on the third ring.

"You wanna go to the mall with us?" Daja said.

"I'm getting my nails done right now. When y'all talkin' 'bout goin', though?" Reka held her free hand up to the light to examine her custom design. "And what mall y'all going to?"

"We thinking about goin' to Southlake, but we might just hit a few of them. So, what's up? You goin'?"

"You still ain't told me when y'all leavin' and who all goin'."

"Me, Alicia, and Tee," Daja said. "And we'll be leaving when you come pick us up. We at Tee's house."

Reka laughed. "You talkin' like y'all already had a ride and shit!"

"We do. You!" Daja laughed. "Isn't that what friends are for?"

"Whatever, bitch. I'll call you when I'm through here at the nail shop. And I hope y'all hos got some money, 'cause my car do not run off air."

84

Triggadale

Daja relayed the message to the background. "Okay, we got some gas money. Just call when you're on your way, 'cause we might not be here."

They ended the call and Reka went back to watching the Asian woman do her nails. Finished, she paid the lady and prepared to leave. "Okay, Kim. I'll be back next week for my fill-in and pedicure. And don't give nobody my design."

The Asian woman smiled, nodding vehemently.

Reka threw on her sunglasses, put her purse on her shoulder, and headed out the door. The sun made her smile as its rays caressed her face.

Yeah, I might need to go to the mall, she thought as she crossed the crowded parking lot.

A car with a couple of guys slowed and blew their horn at her and she smiled, putting an extra sway in her hips. She hit the alarm button on her keychain as she approached her car.

Stepping to the driver's side, she was about to open the door when the side door of a minivan slid open behind her and she was put in a chokehold. She tried to scream, but the tight grip around her neck wouldn't allow a sound to escape as she was snatched off her feet into the van. She kicked and clawed at the arm around her neck, but it was useless.

"Get her keys and purse!" the one holding her neck yelled.

The guy in the passenger seat got out, picked her keys and purse up, and pulled the side door of the van shut, hopping back in the passenger seat. The grip was loosened around Reka's neck and she gasp for air.

"Bitch, if you so much as try to scream, I'ma murk yo' ass!" Her attacker pressed a chrome 9mm to the side of her head as the van started moving.

Forced to lay on the floor, she couldn't see. All that was clear was at least four people were in the van. Sneaking a peek, she realized the one who grabbed her was Marko, the

85

one who questioned her at Tevo's funeral. Fear gripped her like never before.

"Please don't hurt me." Tears filled her eyes, and she began to tremble all over.

As they rode on, no one in the van said anything, and it only added to her fears. She squeezed her eyes shut and said a silent prayer, asking to wake up from this nightmare. Little did she know the nightmare had yet to begin.

Forty-five minutes later she felt the van turn on a gravel road. Five minutes after that, the van turned again and came to a stop. Her legs had gone numb from the position she was lying in, and her neck was aching. The side door opened and she was yanked out of the van by her feet, causing pain to shoot through her body as she hit the ground. The passengers began to unload, and out the corner of her eye she saw her car parked behind the van. The hoarse barks of several dogs could be heard nearby.

"Bitch, stand yo' ass up!" Marko said.

Reka made an attempt to stand, but was snatched up by her arms before she could get to her feet. Taking in her surroundings, she saw she was at an abandoned house surrounded by woods. At that very moment her heart stopped as she experienced fear in its purest form. She couldn't believe her eyes. The house she was staring at was the one that had been in her nightmares.

"No! Please don't hurt me. Please! I'm sorry. They made me do it!" she sobbed. "I loved Tevo."

For her pleas, she was slapped off her feet by Dre. Her vision was blurred and her mouth and nose were bleeding.

"Get her muthsfuckin' ass inside!" Dre ordered.

Marko and another member of the crew carried her inside the old house, stripped off all her clothing, and repeatedly gang-raped her until she was unable to cry. As she lay on the floor in shock, she was sodomized and urinated on. She thought she was hallucinating when she heard the dogs barking again, only this time they were getting closer and closer. She opened her eyes and saw two pitbulls being held by chain leashes as they clawed and scratched to get to her. Her heartbeat proliferated and she squeezed her eyes shut.

I gotta be having another nightmare. This is just another horrible nightmare that I'll be waking up from any minute, she thought.

Lifted from the floor by her hands and feet, she was carried to another room and tossed on the floor. The last thing she saw was the two pitbulls charging toward her. They began biting and shaking her side-to-side. She tried to scream, but couldn't because one had locked onto her throat as Dre closed the door.

"That's for my dawg, bitch!"

Then he walked away.

***

Daja, Alicia, and Tee had called Reka everything except a child of God for not coming to pick them up and ignoring their calls. They figured she was back on that bullshit about falling back from the Mafia. They ended up calling Tall-Teezzee to take them to The Spot. For the rest of the day they kicked shit while a few Mafiosos dropped tracks for an upcoming collaboration mixtape they were putting out. The Mafia had decided to start an independent label called BreakFree Records. The industry had been bucking on signing them due to their notoriety, so they said fuck it. Their first collab would be called *Mafia Muzik: Volume One.*

By nightfall the session was over and all had left except Daja, Alicia, Tee, and two other Mafiosos. Daja checked her phone and saw Reka had yet to call her, and it was after midnight. She tried her number again because she needed a ride home and there was now no one left at The Spot with a car. Baby D and Jayvo left and headed for the club. The phone continued to ring until the voicemail came on.

"Your call has been forwarded to an automated voice message system."

Daja mumbled a few curses and went to wake Alicia and Tee, who had fallen asleep on the living room couch. After waking them, they all began calling different numbers for a ride, but none of them connected with anyone.

"See, that's that bullshit I'm talkin' 'bout, right there!" Daja fumed. "That bitch could at least answer her muthefuckin' phone with her shiesty ass!"

"If she wasn't gon' come pick us up, she should've just said so!" Tee texted away on her phone, furious. "And if I get in trouble for not being at home, I'ma beat her ass. I'm 'pose to be watchin' my li'l brother and sister tomorrow 'til my mama get off work."

They continued to try different numbers, but the results remained the same. No one was picking up.

Two hours later a car pulled into the driveway, and Daja hopped up to look out the window. Huncho and Flame had just pulled up in Flame's Mustang, and Huncho was getting out carrying a book bag on his shoulders. What puzzled Daja was the fact Reka's car was parked in front of the Mustang. Huncho and Flame walked past it and came in the house, curious as to why the porch light wasn't on and where Reka was. It had been a while since she'd shown face at The Spot.

"I don't know. Everybody but us left a couple hours ago. We've been trying to call up a ride. I didn't even know Reka's car was out there." Daja tried the porch light switch by the front door, but nothing happened. "The bulb must be blown."

Huncho sat on the couch and pulled two pounds of purp out of the book bag, setting them on the coffee table. Flame went to the kitchen to find a light bulb. Finding one, he went outside to swap it with the blown one, but noticed the bulb in the socket was halfway screwed out. He screwed it all the way in and went back inside to try the switch. The porch light came right on.

"Man, one of them niggas must've unscrewed the shit while they was sitting out here." Flame stepped back in the living room. "It's all good. I wonder who Reka with, though."

"Y'all don't remember her coming in?" Huncho asked.

"Hell naw, and we been calling her all damn day, so she could've at least woke us up when she came," Daja said. "Matter fact, I'm finna see if she still keep her spare key in the same place. If so she shit outta luck, 'cause I'm driving this bitch home tonight!"

"Drop me off!" Tee quickly added.

"Me too!" Alicia said, following suit.

Daja went outside and felt behind Reka's license plate for the spare key. She pulled back the duct tape, got the key, and walked back around, sticking the key in the door to unlock the driver's side. She opened it and screamed at the top of her lungs, running into the house, shaking and crying, unable to speak.

Huncho and Flame ran out the door with guns in hand. Huncho was leading, and when he got to the car he jumped back as the smell of dry blood and death assaulted his nostrils.

"What the fuck!" Huncho yelled.

Flame walked up to the car to get a better look, and what he saw made him vomit. Reka's mangled, naked, and bloody body was in the front seat, unrecognizable to anyone who knew her.

The two pitbulls had literary torn her apart.

Elijah R. Freeman

Chapter 9

"Southside Mafia is one of Clayton County's fastest-rising gangs." Channel 2 Action News displayed a picture uploaded from MySpace in the upper right-hand corner of the screen. The picture showed several Mafiosos holding AK-47's and different handguns. "They have been suspected in several murders, shootings, and robberies. Since their arrival on the scene, there has been a rise in the gang activity in Riverdale and the surrounding Metro Atlanta area."

It had been a couple of days since Reka was killed, and the heat was on the Mafia like never before. They were constantly being followed around the city wherever they went. Knowing he was public enemy number one, Huncho went underground.

Ring. Ring. Ring.

Huncho muted the television at the sound of his ringing phone, but continued to stare at the screen as he answered. "Yeah, what's up?"

"What you getting into, bra?" asked Flame. "You still in the same place?"

"Yeah, I'm still posted for the moment. Sittin' here checkin' out the news. They talkin' 'bout that shit with Reka, showing pictures and shit."

"Yeah, I just got a call 'bout the same thing. Look though, I'm finna swing through and holla at ya. I don't wanna talk on the phone, feel me?"

"That's a bet."

While he waited on Flame to show up, his mind was on what was going on. He knew the beef with the Squad had just risen ten notches with the murder of Reka. He didn't care how questionable Reka's loyalty had become. There was no way it could go unanswered when it had been broadcast on the news every day, all day. If the Mafia didn't avenge her death, the respect they had on the street would be lost. They would be looked at as weak for not riding for one of their own, and the Mafia wasn't going out like that.

Huncho shook his head slowly, running his hand through his dreads. Wasn't a day gone by he didn't think about the night he was shot. He could still see the flames spit from the barrel, the look on Dre's face. Some days it made him so mad he would unknowingly bite down on his lip until he tasted blood. Killing Dre was his objective, and he wouldn't rest until he accomplished his mission.

"Are you hungry?" Camry stood at the living room's entrance. Her parents went out of town, leaving her the house, so Huncho had been spending his nights over there. She was happy he was there and not in the streets, so she was trying her best to make him comfortable.

"Daldrick, are you hungry?" she asked a second time after receiving no answer.

He snapped from his thoughts. "Yeah, what you cookin'?"

"Some chicken fingers and fries."

"Yeah, I'll take some."

Halfway through his meal, Flame arrived and Camry reluctantly let him in. She knew there was a chance of Huncho leaving as long as he was around. With much attitude, she stormed off to her bedroom.

"Shoota say 12 been watchin' The Spot." Flame grabbed a few fries from Huncho's plate. "He say they been sitting on the side of the road, taking pictures and shit. He think the old bitch next door got something to do with it, too, 'cause her nosey-ass stay lookin' over there, tryna see what's goin' on. I think we need a new spot."

"Probably so." Huncho stuck the last chicken finger in his mouth. "Who all been stayin' over there lately?"

"J-Rock, Jayvo, and Baby-D mostly, and they be havin' a few hos stayin' wit' 'em."

"They dirty?"

"Naw, they got all the weed somewhere else, and ain't but two tools in the house. They put up good, though."

Huncho took a deep swallow of the Kool-Aid Camry made to go with his meal. "Just tell 'em to keep the traffic low-key until the heat die down. We don't need them folks running up in there."

After yelling to Camry that he would be outside, he walked out on the back patio with Flame, wearing black Dickie shorts, a black tank top, and black Nike socks with no shoes, a 9mm tucked in his waistline. He passed the blunt to Flame while he smoked a cigarette.

"What I wanted to holla at you 'bout was a lick I peeped the other day," Flame said with raised eyebrows.

Huncho shook his head, flicked the half Newport away, and reached for the blunt. "Run it by me, and it better not be no bullshit!"

Flame gave him the rundown, and Huncho quickly agreed. Later that night he came to pick Huncho up and they went to hit the lick.

The lick was at a female's house who Flame had been seeing. Her father had a collection of guns in a cabinet and throughout the house. Huncho waited outside the house until Flame and the girl went to get something to eat at a nearby McDonald's. He then entered through a back window Flame left unlocked before departing. He knew exactly where everything was from Flame searching the house during one of his earlier visits, so it was a get-and-go job. Ten minutes and two trips later, Huncho had sixteen guns hidden in the bushes. To throw the heat off Flame, he busted a window on the door on his way out to make it seem like forced entry.

When Flame picked him up after dropping the girl off, he had an SKS, AR-15, two pistol grip pumps, and twelve different handguns that they stashed at Camry's house, despite her protests.

"Them fuck-niggas gon' feel it, sho nuff now!" Huncho raised the AR-15 to his shoulder and looked through the night vision scope, smiling.

***

Brandi and Shea were coming out McDonald's on Highway 85 when they bumped into Tee and Katrina. At first it was a stare down until Tee recognized Shea from the beat down she helped put on her and started laughing, reminding her friend of the incident.

"What them hos find so funny?" Brandi asked Shea.

"I don't know," Shea said.

"Well, we sho 'bout to find out." Brandi turned to address the snickering females. "Y'all hos know us from somewhere?"

"Naw, bitch, should we?" Katrina said.

"Naw, bitch. You can get to know us, though!" Brandi shot back, pulling her braids back into a ponytail.

Shea stood beside Brandi, ready for the rumble as Meeka and Zaria got out of the car, hurrying over to the standoff. Customers walked past the foul-mouthed girls cursing back and forth at each other, and before long things were heating up.

Brandi ran up on Katrina and they started bumping chests and pointing fingers in each other's faces until Meeka reached over Brandi's shoulder and punched Katrina in the face, remembering her as one of the girls who jumped her before. Brandi followed up with several blows, swinging her arms like a windmill. Katrina ducked her head, swinging back, but that turned out to be a mistake. Brandi grabbed her hair and snatched as hard as she could, causing Katrina to scream out in pain as she crashed face-first to the ground. Shea and Zaria were double-teaming Tee, who they had on the ground between

94

two cars. kicking and stomping her like they had literally gone mad.

A crowd gathered, watching the brawl from inside McDonald's, but they all scattered when Yana hopped out of the car brandishing a .25 automatic. She aimed the small gun at Shea's back, unbeknownst to her, as she and Zaria continued to stomp Tee out. Two quick shots and Shea fell forward, the others freezing at the sound of gunfire. Yana looked down at Shea, who had fallen on top of Tee and was leaking blood profusely.

"Yeah, bitch! Southside Queens, ho!" She raised her gun to fire at a panic-struck Zaria, who had taken off running with Brandi.

Pop! Pop! Pop! Pop!

The small .25 sounded off as she chased behind Brandi and Zaria, letting off shot after shot, shattering windows and causing car alarms to go off as the slugs hit parked cars. Meeka had also abandoned the beat-down she and Brandi had been administering to Katrina, but they had run in the opposite direction, taking cover in McDonald's.

"Call 911! My friend's been shot!" she screamed as she ran through the doors.

Two Clayton County squad cars whipped into the McDonald's parking lot, sirens blaring. Seeing Yana toting a gun, both officers jumped out and pointed their guns, demanding she drop hers.

"Drop your weapon! Now!" The officers were ducked behind the doors of their cruisers, guns trained on Yana. "Drop it now and raise your hands!"

Yana dropped her gun and complied with the officers' commands. More officers flooded the parking lot from all directions, jumping out with their shotguns and pistols in hand, advancing on Yana, who was now facing the reality of what she just did. She was ordered to lie face down and lock her hands behind her head.

Elijah R. Freeman

Shea lay on the ground screaming and crying in a puddle of her own blood as the burning sensation from the two bullets spread throughout her body. Meeka ran out of the McDonald's and over to Shea, screaming for help. Several officers ran over, and within minutes Shea was being treated by EMS workers and transported to the hospital.

***

Gotti pulled up at the HQ on Grove Street and went in the house with two cases of 211, a twelve-pack under each arm. *Diesel Truck*, a recent H.S.T. track, blared from the speakers, and the house was thick with smoke when he entered. He passed Kebo, Cap, and Frog playing Saints Row on the Xbox and dapped D. Moss up on the couch, passing a twelve-pack to Waka. There was a spades game going on in the kitchen. From there he could see some more of his homeboys gathered on the patio where the grill was smoking.

He stepped out onto the patio with two beers. Dre was standing in front of the grill with a long fork in his hand.

"Aye, shawdy, I just heard Shea got shot!"

"Got shot?" Dre said. "How the fuck she get shot?"

Gotti passed him a beer, opening one for himself. "Her, Brandi, Meeka, and Zaria got into it with them Queen hos. They say one of 'em had a tool and busted her twice in the back while she was stompin' one of them bitches out."

"Damn, where they was at?"

Gotti sipped the foam from the beer. "At the McDonald's on 85. Meeka called me a couple minutes ago from the hospital. Say the ho was bustin' at her, too, but she ran."

"Damn, that's fucked up." Dre took a swallow of his beer. Since killing Reka and leaving her body at The Spot, Dre had a feeling of invincibility. He was mistaking the

96

Mafia laying low due to the investigation as fear from the way he left Reka's body. The Squad looked at him with more respect, and some even feared him after what he'd done. The murder relieved him somewhat, but he wanted real relief, and that would only come from killing Huncho and watching him die for taking his twin brother's life.

As the night went on, H.S.T. got even more fucked up as they sat around the house drinking and smoking. A couple of females came through to join them as well.

"Y'all still beefing with Southside Mafia?" one of the females asked.

"Beef? What beef? Them pussy-ass niggas hiding somewhere. They don't wanna see us!" Dre was drunk, but bold. "Matta fact, I'd 'preciate it if you didn't e'en mention them fuck-boys 'round me no more!"

"Well, I was asking because I heard this guy that go to Riverdale High School talking 'bout how Huncho killed your brother and how you shot him, or some shit like that."

At the mention of his brother, his face twisted up. "And when I find that fuck-nigga, he's dead! That's why his bitch-ass hiding now." He took another swallow of beer. Angry, he continued to talk recklessly about what he was going to do to the Mafia and Huncho, boasting about how Hit Squad Taliban was the real mob and how Huncho and his crew were imposters and wannabes. He claimed H.S.T. was the hottest thing in the streets, not knowing the whole time he was boasting and bragging to the enemy.

The four females who had been coming over for the last week were Southside Queens. Huncho and Flame sent them to infiltrate the Squad so they would know when and where to strike when the heat died. The Mafia was preparing for war during a time of peace to ensure when they did hit, they would wipe their enemy out.

The four females left when Dre fell asleep. They called Flame and Huncho as they pulled away, telling them everything that was going on and everything that was said.

***

Yana sat in the empty room, nervous, cold, and scared. She had been sitting for over an hour. When the detectives first tried to question her, she wouldn't cooperate at all. They knew she was a member of the Southside Queens from the SSQ tattoo on her wrist. They made promises, and even after they threatened to charge her with murder, claiming Shea was dead, it still didn't work.

Now she was ready to go. She was tired, hungry, and sick of sitting stiff in the hard, uncomfortable chair. The wall she had up was starting to fall. She got up and started pacing back and forth, stopping every now and then when she heard a voice or keys jingling on the other side of the door. She had stuck her arms inside her shirt to keep warm, and the more she paced and waited, the more she began to regret what she had done.

Is the girl I shot really dead? she wondered. *If so, that means I might never go home again.*

She heard keys at the door and jumped as it came open. The detective who called himself Ellis stuck his head in the door and told her to have a seat as he and another detective stepped in. She sat.

"Here, I brought you this. You want it?" Ellis sat a package of malt crackers and a Sprite on the table in front of her.

"Thank you." She grabbed the crackers and Sprite.

Ellis took a seat across from Yana while the other detective opted to stand. "You feel like talking yet? Because if not, I can go back to my desk and finish up some paperwork. I don't get off until six in the morning."

Yana washed the dry crackers down with the cold Sprite, unable to remember one ever tasting so good. She thought about what the detective just said. She didn't know what time it was, but she knew six o'clock in the morning was a long way away.

She ate another cracker. "Yeah, I guess so."

After questioning her about the shooting at the McDonald's for over an hour and getting her to confess she had done it, he went into another series of questions all about Southside Mafia. She was the first member of the gang he could get to cooperate, and he knew he had to get all he could out of her. He took his time, speaking with her calmly as if he was a friend or father figure. He even lied, saying he was once in a gang and understood.

"So, I see you know a lot about Southside Mafia," he said. "Well, let me ask ya, do you know a guy named Huncho?"

Yana nodded slowly. "Yeah. He's 7675, but I know him."

"They originated off Lyle Drive, right?"

Again, Yana nodded.

"You have to speak up so the recorder will pick you up. I might have to go back and listen to this," he smiled. "It's like my notepad, 'cause my memory isn't as good as it used to be. I hear Huncho is a pretty bad boy. You ever heard of him shooting anybody?"

She hesitated for a second, uncertain if she should answer the question. "Do I have to answer that?"

"It would help a lot if you did, and right now you need all the help you can get." Ellis knew he had his fish on the hook, and he was reeling it in.

"Well," she smacked her lips. "Yeah, he shot a guy at Sparkles one night. I heard that's why he was shot at a football game. The shooter was the first guy's brother. I think they were twins."

Detective Ellis shifted in his seat. "Hold on, let's go back to the one at Sparkles. Were you there when it happened?"

"Yes, I was there. We were at Sparkles in Riverdale," she said. "Some boys from Grove Street –"

"I-I'm sorry, from where?" Ellis asked, cutting her off.

"Well, Riverdale Road, but everyone calls it Grove Street," she said. "Anyways, some boys from there jumped Nard in the parking lot, and he shot one of them with a shotgun and killed him. Flame gave my friend the gun and told her to leave with it, so she did what he said and got in the backseat with it in my – well, my mama's car."

Detective Ellis waited a few seconds, acting as if he was writing on the pad in front of him before speaking again. "But did you see him shoot this guy at Sparkles?"

"Yes, I saw him do it."

Ellis nodded. "Anything else you'd like to tell me that might can help?"

"He had this girl named Reka. Well, him and Flame had Reka set one of the Hit Squad boys up, and I heard they killed him inside of this old house and cut his head off."

Ellis looked up from his notepad, surprised. He suddenly remembered the gruesome scene inside the car at the crime scene on Lyle Drive. "Are you talking about Eureka Stephens?"

"Yes, that's her," Yana said. "She's dead, too."

"So, Huncho and this guy Flame had her set someone up that ended up dead in a house with their head cut off."

"Yes. It was two more girls with her, too."

"Here, I want you to write down everything you know, and include all the names, especially the two females you just mentioned. I'm going to leave you alone for a few minutes so you can concentrate, okay? Just take your time and try to remember all you can. Do you want some chips or a candy bar? I know you might be hungry."

She nodded and both detectives left the room with smiles on their faces as they headed to their desks to call a magistrate judge and get murder warrants for Huncho and

Flame. The judge authorized the warrants, and they got them signed after dropping Yana back off at the jail.

Elijah R. Freeman

Chapter 10

Shea underwent several excisions to remove the bullets from her back, but only one was successfully extracted. Too close to her spine, doctors felt it best to leave the second bullet be, predicting she'd be paralyzed from the waist down. The bullet had damaged some nerves.

For three days she'd been in Southern Regional, her mother and friends by her bedside. She hadn't been told she was paralyzed. Her mother and doctor felt it best to let her get a little better before breaking the news to her. Detectives had been back and forth to question her, but were unsuccessful due to her heavy sedation. The doctors advised the detectives that it would be too traumatic for her to relive the event so early and made them leave, promising to give them a call whenever she was discharged.

Shea awoke in the hospital, eyes squinting from the light. The first thing she saw was her mother looking down, smiling as she smoothed her hair back.

"How you feeling, baby?" she said.

"Not too good." Slowly, Shea looked left and right, taking in all the gifts, flowers, cards, and balloons that filled the room. She yawned. "It hurts all over, and I can't feel my legs. Did I get shot in my legs?"

"No, baby. You didn't."

"Then what's wrong with me?"

"Nothing's wrong, dear. You're fine," she lied. "The feeling will come back soon."

Brandi, Meeka, and Zaria walked in, smiling with balloons and flowers in hand. Shea lit up, and at the sight her mother smiled as well. She chatted along with the girls for a minute, then left to get something to eat.

In her absence, more serious topics were discussed as they brought Shea up to date with the latest on the gossip

---

mill. It was obvious their presence lifted her spirits. As Meeka braided her hair, they gave her an update on Yana.

"She still locked up. Safest place for her, too, from what I hear."

"What you mean?"

"They say she snitched on Huncho and that boy Flame he be with," Brandi said. "12 been runnin' up in everybody shit looking for them. They wanted for killing Taliban. And I wanna say Tevo, too."

"I thought I saw them on the news. I only saw their pictures, but I figured I dreamed it," Shea said.

They went on about everything under the sun until Shea began to doze off from the medication. Shea's mother returned, thanked Meeka for braiding Shea's hair, and they left, leaving the two of them together.

Back home, they found out Dre had been arrested along with several other Squad affiliates when police raided one of their hangouts. Guns had been found, along with two bulletproof vests and a drug stash.

***

The Spot had been raided twice by heavily-armed SWAT officers looking for Huncho, who first learned of the murder warrant when his mother called, cursing him out after the Fugitive Task Force stormed her house at 4:30 in the morning. Two days later his face was on every local news station in the Metro area. Flame, who was said to be an accomplice, was wanted also.

With the streets on fire, they held up the Phillips 66 at the light where 8800 Block met Valley Hill, striking for sixteen hundred apiece. That wasn't enough for them, though. Not for fugitives on the run with bodies. Playing it safe, they rid themselves of Flame's Mustang, rented a red Chrysler 300, and took heavily to robbing. They were all but playing. Give it up or get shot. It was just that simple. Living on borrowed time had them on go-mode.

A few stick-ups later, they hit the road. Flame suggested his cousin Tony's residence in Griffin, and that's where they headed. Lying low in Backline, they spotted plenty of potential victims to touch before leaving for the next scene. Tony pointed out licks for them as well, but Huncho didn't trust him. He talked too much and thought he had more game than the Sports Center.

Huncho thought it best to relocate, but Flame assured him they were good. Tony smoked dope, but he would never cross family. Huncho let it die, but he kept a close eye on Tony at all times. He got a bad vibe from him, and the feeling was mutual. The money and drugs they gave him were the only reasons he wasn't complaining. Every time he got high, he felt unsafe around Huncho. The bulletproof vest, the two pistols on him 24/7, it made him uncomfortable.

Two weeks in Backline and Huncho was ready to swerve. Their money was low, and he was officially bored with their surroundings. Not to mention the weed they got from Ski and Nard was gone, leaving them stuck smoking the bullshit Spaulding County weed. Huncho addressed the issue and, to his surprise, Flame's attitude mirrored his own. It was settled. They were out of there, Flame just didn't know where to. Anywhere, for all Huncho cared. All they needed now was to run up some "anywhere" money.

At ten o'clock that night, part two of their robbing spree began. To avoid unwanted heat, they invaded the homes of local drug dealers, demanding cash and work in exchange for their families' lives. Buck the jack? Yeah, right.

Flame knocked on the door of their final victim for the night. It was one of Tony's moves and was supposed to be big. Just as he'd done with the first couple of spots they hit, Huncho stood off to the side gripping a black .40 cal in each hand. A voice asked who it was from the other side, and Flame gave them the name given to him by Tony.

The door curtain slid to the side, and the face of an ugly, overweight, Rick Ross prototype appeared in the window, asking again for a name. Flame repeated himself, this time backing his face card with another A-1 shopper.

The door opened, and in the foyer stood a mean-muggin', sandwich-clutching fat guy with no shirt and a pair of black basketball shorts.

Huncho rushed him to the floor, giving Flame free reign to shoot to the back. Kicking the door shut behind him, he made Fat Boy lay on his stomach in the living room. Putting the pistol to his head, Huncho demanded the work and money, but Fat Boy played dumb, claiming to make an honest living.

A woman screamed from a back room, and moments later Flame returned with Fat Boy's wife and kids. When asked about the work and money again, Fat Boy sang a different song. There was a wall safe in his study behind a painting of Augustine Clayton in which he kept two and a half bricks and 35 large.

They left the house, walking with a purpose. Down the street, they hopped in the rental and headed straight for the expressway.

"I need to grab them guns from Camry's house." Huncho flicked the blinker, switching lanes. "After that, we headed to Alabama."

"Alabama!" Flame looked at Huncho like he was crazy. "Who the fuck you know in Alabama?"

Huncho smiled. "Nobody, but we got two and a half bricks to get off, and I heard the money was good down there."

***

Triggadale

Dre had been home from the County Jail for three days. News of Huncho and Flame's murder warrants had him anxious. They were the talk of Riverdale. Dre didn't want the police to catch them, though. He had a different kind of justice in mind. A permanent one.

Since Tevo's murder, Dre and Brandi had grown close. When she asked him to ride with her to Southern Regional to see Shea, he agreed. They kicked it with Shea for an hour and a half until the nurse came and administered her medication. On their way out, they ran into Ellis and Foster, who stopped to speak to Brandi. Coincidentally, they were on their way to see Shea. Uneasy in their presence, Dre shuffled around, trying to avoid eye contact.

"You staying out of trouble, young lady?" Ellis was familiar with Brandi, having questioned her on a few occasions.

She smiled. "Yes, I'm a good girl."

"How's she doing in there?"

"A lot better, actually," Brandi said, "but she was just going to sleep, so we were leaving."

Foster eyed Dre, taking note of his discomfort the entire time they'd been talking. Ellis caught on and turned his attention to him, sticking out his hand with a smile. "How're you doing, young man?" No response. "I'm Detective Ellis. And you are?"

Dre looked down at the offered hand. He had never shaken hands with the police, not to mention a detective. The Glock 40 on his waistline started to feel as if it weighed a ton and was slipping down his leg. His palms began to sweat, and he wiped them on his pants leg before shaking Ellis's hand.

"I'm fine, sir."

It didn't get by Ellis that he hadn't mentioned his name. "You staying out of trouble, aren't you?" Ellis stared him dead in the eyes. "This is a nice young lady you're with."

"Oh yes, sir. I don't get in trouble. I'm tryna go to the NBA," he lied.

"Well, that's good to hear. And what did you say your name was again?"

Dre said the first name that came to mind. "Rico."

The look on Brandi's face gave him away, but the detectives didn't pry any further. They knew he was lying, and if he was lying, that could mean only one thing: he was hiding something.

Away from the detectives, Dre speed-walked until they were out of sight. On the elevator, he pulled Brandi close to him, and to her surprise he pulled the Glock from his waist, then stuffed it in her purse. Seeing what he was doing, she relaxed and stayed close to him. So close she could feel his nature rising against her booty. She had never looked at Dre in a sexual way due to her messing with Tevo, but what she felt at that moment was something totally new.

They exited the elevator, heading to the parking lot. The entire ride home was in silence.

Back at the hospital, Ellis was wrapping up his interview with Shea. As he and Foster were standing to leave, they thanked her for her cooperation and apologized for waking her.

Ellis snapped and pointed. "Oh yeah, I bumped into your two friends on my way in. Uh. Brandi and, what's that fellow's name again? He told me, but it slipped my mind while talking to you."

"Dre," Shea yawned.

"Oh yeah, that's right. Dre. Dre, uh?" He fake-tried to remember a last name.

"Chambers." She closed her eyes. "Deandre Chambers."

The detectives left the room and Ellis stopped on the other side of the door, turning to face Foster. "Liar! I knew he looked familiar."

"And you know him from?" Foster asked.

108

"Deandre Chambers. Name doesn't ring a bell?" Foster shook his head. "The kid Blanding murdered at Sparkles. Doesn't he have a twin brother."

"Well, I'll be damned. Small world, isn't it?" Foster smiled. "I wonder what he's hiding to make him give us a fake name?"

"It shouldn't be too hard to figure out. Think about it. If Blanding and Southside Mafia are responsible for the death of his twin brother and possibly a member of his crew, I know what he's hiding."

Foster's mouth dropped. "He's the one who shot Blanding."

Ellis nodded. "That's not all. More than likely he's responsible for the girl found dead in the car, too. According to our informant, she was the one who set up Gaines. It's all coming together. If my gut feeling is right, Tevin Gaines, or Tevo, was Deandre's friend. Come on, let's go."

***

Camry stood in the dark, tears streaming down her face and glistening in the moonlight. She and Huncho were in her parent's backyard, surrounded by the sounds of mating crickets. It was after three in the morning.

Earlier, Huncho sent a text explaining what he needed done with the guns he left. Parking two streets over in another subdivision, he hit the cut and hopped the fence that led to her house. Chances were Camry was being watched, thus his reason for taking the extra precautions.

"I need you to get this to Ma Dukes A.S.A.P." Huncho handed Camry a Wendy's bag, in which was $25,000 and a letter. "And here go something for yo'self, too. I'm finna leave town for a while. Tell Ma Dukes that money is for me for a lawyer. I need the best one she can find."

Did he exactly trust his mother? No. But he rationalized that whenever he seemed to be in extreme danger, she showed face, if nothing else. He just hoped he could count on her now. However, if she did decide to run off with the money, at least when he went down he knew she would have something.

He was a surprised to find he gave a damn, but he did.

"What about the baby, Daldrick? I need for you to be here with me." Camry looked up at him. "Why don't you just turn yourself in and get it over with, baby?"

"I can't."

"Why?"

"I just–I just can't right now, shawdy." He took her in his arms and she broke down. "Take care of yoself, okay?"

She nodded.

He was already taking a chance being there and needed to be on his way, but he also knew this could be his last time seeing his baby mama. He rubbed her stomach and they kissed long and passionately like it was their first time.

"Now go in the house, baby." He forced himself to step back. "I got to go."

She stood crying, staring at him. She wasn't going to move. Seeing this, he turned and headed for the cut.

"I love you, Daldrick!" she said in a voice laced with sorrow.

Huncho stopped mid-stride and looked back. "I love you more." Then he continued toward the cut carrying the guns. When he got to the car, Flame cursed him out for taking so long and they headed to the expressway.

They were off to Alabama.

Chapter 11

The next day, Yana bonded out of the Clayton County Detention Center and was picked by her mother. They went out to eat at American Deli on S.R. 138 where they held a strained conversation due to her mother not wanting to argue. She knew any mention of Yana not hanging out with Southside Queens anymore would cause an argument, so she refrained from speaking on the topic.

As soon as they made it home, Yana showered and began calling her homegirls. She figured there was no way they could possibly know she ratted out Huncho and Flame. Her first call was to Katrina who, unbeknownst to her, had already been put on game about her dime dropping, but was told to play it cool. Answering her phone, she gave no indication of her knowledge and did just that.

"So, when did you get home?" she asked. "'Cause, girl, I thought yo' ass was gone."

"A couple hours ago. My mama bonded me out and came to pick me up," Yana said. "So, what's been going on since I been off the scene?"

Katrina decided to test the waters. "Well, you heard about Huncho and Flame, didn't you?"

"No, what happened, girl? You know I ain't talked to nobody but you since I been out."

Katrina wasn't hoodwinked by her display of surprise. She already knew what she had done, but if she hadn't known beforehand that Yana was a snitch, she would've been fooled. *This bitch is good*, she thought.

It didn't take a rocket scientist to figure out what happened. All it took was a little deductive reasoning. Yana gets cased up and all of a sudden Huncho and Flame are on the run for a murder they hadn't previously been tied to. It was all circumstantial, but logical. The call had been made. Yana was a dead bitch walking.

"They on the run for murder," Katrina said. "They pictures been on the news and everything."

"Oh my god, you for real? Who they killed, girl?"

Katrina frowned on the other end of the phone at her fakeness because Yana knew who they killed. She was there. And even if she wasn't, she still would've known due to her affiliation with the Mafia or, if nothing else, the streets talking.

She caught herself before answering as the thought crossed her mind that Yana might have the police on the phone. "Girl, I don't know. You know how people in the streets be talking and making shit up. But what you doing? You coming out to celebrate your release? I know Tee gon' be glad to see yo' ass after the way you saved her from getting stomped out."

They shared a laugh, talking briefly about the fight and her shooting Shea. Katrina couldn't lie, Yana used to put on for the Queens. She couldn't believe of all people, she folded.

"Well, I guess I'll come out. But y'all gotta come pick me up because my mama ain't givin' me the keys to her car no time soon."

Thirty minutes later Yana was headed out of the house, hopping in the car with Katrina, Daja, and Tee. Behind them were four more Queens in another car who smiled and waved as she got in the back seat. They laughed and talked, giving her props for how she stood tall for the Mafia.

They pulled up at The New Spot and she was greeted with hugs and love, getting all of the attention as blunt after blunt and cup after cup were passed to her. Two hours in she was seeing double, unable to stand on her own. Her speech was slurred and she was so drunk she began to cry for no reason, vehemently expressing how much love she had for the Mafia. Had she been sober, she would've seen

112

no one was smiling anymore. Everyone stared with mean mugs and screw faces, waiting on her to fall asleep.

Soon enough, she did just that.

"Yana!" Katrina was holding a phone to her ear. "Can you hear me, Yana?"

Yana shook her head as tears flowed from her eyes. She tried to raise her hands to push the phone away, but couldn't. They were tied behind her back.

This has to be a nightmare, she told herself.

The voice came clearer than before. "Guess what, Yana," the voice said. "You finna die, you snitching-ass bitch! Hope you ain't too drunk to say your prayers and ask God to forgive you, because I won't!"

It was Huncho.

Katrina pulled the phone away with a smile and brought it to her ear as Yana began sobbing, repeating over and over how sorry she was. "Yeah, Huncho, what's up?"

Everyone else stood by silently, watching and waiting.

"After you handle that, I want y'all to get back on them Hit Squad Taliban niggas." As Huncho spoke, Katrina snapped her finger and pointed at Yana. "I'll be calling from a new number, but I don't know when, so make sure your line is clear."

Missy put a plastic bag over Yana's head and duct taped it around her neck so no air could get in. Yana resisted, but it was useless. Her hands and feet were also duct taped. All she could do was wiggle and jerk as she suffocated.

***

At that exact same moment, Yana's mother was knocking on her door, calling her name. She opened the door and saw Yana was not there, as she thought. Shaking her head, she walked over and turned off the stereo that was

113

left blaring. She sat on the bed, looking at the open window her daughter had snuck out of.

***

Detective Ellis got to the jail too late to question Yana about Dre's involvement in everything that was going on. He knew if he could connect Dre with Tevo and learn their relationship, he would more than likely have Reka's killer. He already had a motive for Dre shooting Huncho.

Learning that Yana made bond that morning, he went back to his office in Jonesboro on North McDonough Street Once at his office, he got on his computer, pulled up Dre's record, and printed it with a picture of him. He then tracked down Yana's personal information and wrote her phone number and address down. He picked up the phone and was about to call until he looked out the window and caught a glimpse of how beautiful the day was. He hung up, deciding against cold calling and opting to pay her a personal visit instead.

Around the corner from Riverdale Park, he pulled into her driveway on Grayson Street. A couple knocks later, a middle-aged woman in a lavender robe answered the door.

"How may I help you?" Her voice was soft.

"Hi, I'm Detective Ellis. I was looking for Iona Davis."

Brows creased, she pulled her robe a little tighter. "Well, I'm her mother. Is everything okay? What seems to be the problem?"

"She's not in any trouble. I just wanted to ask her a few more questions. I'm the detective assigned to her case."

"Well, she's not here right now. And to be honest, Mr. Ellis, I don't know where she is. I picked her up from jail, and when we came home she took a shower then snuck back out the house without me knowing, and I haven't heard from her since."

Triggadale

They conversed for another fifteen minutes and he left, leaving her with a card and instructions to call as soon as she heard from Yana. As he drove back to headquarters, his mind was on the cases.

***

Huncho and Flame had been in Emelle, Alabama on the outskirts of Mississippi for three days, peeping the scene. They found the old country town after searching for the place where most black people congregated. After going to a club in neighboring Geiger, they were directed to Emelle. Their plan was to lay low there for a minute and sell the two and a half bricks they had in the surrounding cities.

They met two females at a hole-in-the-wall club: Monica and Tip. They turned out to be cousins who stayed in the Emelle area. After a night of club flossin', they followed them. They arrived in Emelle and got Tip to rent a room in her name for a week. They spent the rest of the night with them, getting the rundown of the city and intel on where shit was popping. Peeping the drought, they set up shop instead of traveling back to Birmingham as they had originally planned.

They made their first sell to Monica's brother five days later, charging him $1,200 for an ounce of cocaine. Within 45 minutes he was back for more. They knew they could've charged him more being that they were in the country, but to them it was free money, and they were only trying to get off the free work.

The guy they were dealing with was Gator. They made it clear to him he was the only one they wanted to see or deal with. His first visit to the room he saw the two assault rifles that sat next to them and Huncho in the bulletproof vest, not to mention the two pistols they each carried. He realized early on they were not to be crossed. Re-up after re-up, it was the same thing. Good business.

Pretty soon Gator was copping work by the nines, spending ten racks every trip. Being from the city, Huncho and Flame knew they could tax a country nigga, but Gator was still getting a playa deal. They put nothing on the work. It was straight off the block, clean coke, no oil base, so ten stacks for a quarter key sounded like music to his ears.

Money counted, Flame grabbed the scale and began to throw pieces of rocked-up coke on it. The entire time Huncho sat quietly on the bed, M16 laying across his lap. It was the same scene every deal that transpired. Like most, Gator never felt comfortable in Huncho's presence.

Finished handling business with Gator, they went to the other room connected to theirs, but rented in a different name. They had paid the maid to get someone to rent it for them. They also paid the maid fifty dollars a day to be their eyes and ears, a small price to pay for the peace of mind it brought. They made it look to Gator like the room he visited was the one they stayed in. Monica and Tip knew nothing of their second room, either.

"Bra, this shit be beating, don't it?" Flame re-counted the money and split it down the middle.

"Hell yeah. That half 'bout gone, ain't it?" Huncho sized up the leftover work. "Just imagine if we stayed down here and had a plug back home. We'd be rich in no time!"

Flame nodded, handing Huncho his half. "We got enough for our lawyers, and with that bitch Yana out the way, we might stand a chance. What you think?"

Huncho pondered the question, absentmindedly fanning out his bankroll. "All depends on what that bitch told them folks and if anybody else is snitchin'."

That night they hit the strip club, dressed in all black, rocking iced-out pieces they had snagged from some of the Griffin robberies. Off the rip they received stares, instantly recognized as out-of-towners. Once the dancers found out where they were from, they flocked to them, leaving the

116

regulars looking on in envy as they did them. No cares. No worries. They threw money at the strippers as if they printed it themselves, had bottles sent to their table, females on their laps as others danced in front of them, the whole nine.

Gator walked in the club around midnight. Noticing them, he came over to greet them. In doing so he solved the enigma that had been created at their initial arrival on the scene. Everyone was wondering where Gator was getting all the work from. He was making two ounces out of every one he got, so the quarter brick was stepped on and turned into half a brick, making him the man overnight in the small town.

"I see ya folks ain't looking too happy in here," Flame yelled over the blaring music.

Gator shrugged. "Man, fuck these broke-ass niggas. They ain't gon' do shit."

"But get killed thinking this shit sweet!" Huncho said. Gator looked over at him, getting the vibe the comment was for him as well.

With four strippers, Huncho, Flame, and Gator left the club to cold stares from a group in the parking lot. They were tipsy, but not enough to miss the animosity. Huncho had snuck a small compact nine in the club by sticking it in his pocket, so when he peeped the crowd and the way they were staring, he put his hand in his pocket.

"Damn, Gator, you don't know us no more, huh?" somebody yelled from the crowd.

Gator laughed it off and continued walking toward his money-green Suburban. A second later a bottle crashed behind them. Huncho stopped and spun around. In front of their car, Flame quickly unlocked the doors and grabbed his two pistols from under the car seat.

"Don't throw it and hide ya hand, fuck-nigga!" Huncho yelled. "Be a man about it."

"Ya betta getcha li'l skinny ass in that car 'fore you get kicked ta sleep out cha. You must not know where the fuck you at?" a guy from the crew said, gaining laughs from the crowd.

"You dead-ass right, bra." Huncho turned to Flame, pushing him back toward the car. "Crank the car up, bra."

Mistaking Huncho turning away and heading to the car for backing down, more people in the crowd began to speak up.

"I'ma meet y'all at the room, shawdy." He told Gator and the strippers, who got in the Suburban and pulled off.

The crowd was in the middle of the parking lot, issuing threats as they headed their way. Flame popped the trunk for Huncho when he got to the back of the car, and he snatched up the choppa with the hundred-round drum. Cocking it, he stepped back to the front of the car.

"Nigga, fuck where I'm at! It's still Triggadale, pussy nigga!" He raised the choppa and fired off thirty quick rounds as the crowd scattered. He hopped back in the car, laughing as Flame mashed his foot on the gas. He had only shot in the air to let the crowd know what it could've been if they wanted to crank up the fuck-shit.

"That was just to let ya know Southside Mafia in town, nigga!" he yelled out the window.

As they passed some of the ones who scattered to hide behind cars, he emptied the compact nine in the air, laughing.

Chapter 12

David Mitchell worked third shift at a warehouse in Jonesboro. He was on his way home after a long night and a couple hours of overtime. He cracked both front windows as he drove to allow cool air inside his truck, something he did to keep him awake while driving. He had been at his job for over fifteen years, taking the same route he was now for just as long.

Sitting at the red light on Highway 85 behind a few cars, he wished the light would change. Three more turns and he would be pulling into his driveway.

One left, two rights, and then I can relax at last, he thought with a sigh.

The light finally changed and he glanced at the burgundy "Welcome to Riverdale" sign posted in front of the Chevron, before he made a left onto S.R. 138. It made him think of Riverdale High School, where his son would be graduating at the end of the school year. He was so proud of him and didn't mind putting in overtime hours to send him off to a good college. It was his duty as a father.

He slowed and made a right on Grayson Street. *Almost there now*, he thought blissfully.

Suddenly, he slammed on the brakes, his chest straining against the seatbelt before he was thrown back into his seat. "What the?" He rose up on his steering wheel, looking over the dash into the street. He cut on his high beams. Seeing it was a person lying in the street, he got out. *Maybe they got drunk, stumbled, and fell,* he thought, approaching the figure in the street.

"Oh my God! Lord have mercy!" He began to step back when he saw the person lying in the street had a bag over their head and duct tape on both wrists and ankles.

He turned, ran to his truck, and pulled out his phone to call 911 and report what he saw. He explained to them how he stumbled upon the body and homicide detectives were immediately called out to the crime scene. He got his gun out of the glove compartment and sat it on his lap until the first police arrived on the scene.

***

Detective Ellis was asleep when he got the call. Hearing it was an unidentified black female who looked to be in her late teens or early twenties, he told them he was en route and not to process the scene until he got there. It took him a little over thirty minutes to arrive. By that time the houses in the neighborhood were lit up and both sides of the streets were lined with squad cars.

A uniformed cop was just finishing putting up a perimeter of yellow crime scene tape. From what he could see, there were no numbered evidence tents to mark the presence of any shell cases on the ground, so a shooting wasn't the case. What made his heart drop was when he pulled up and saw the body lay in front of the house he visited earlier, and the lady he had spoken to stood on the sidewalk with neighbors, crying.

"What do we have?" He walked toward the crime scene led by another detective. They ducked under the yellow crime scene tape and started toward the body that was covered with a white sheet.

"We have what appears to be a young African-American female, late teens or early twenties, but it's hard to be sure because a plastic bag has been taped over her head."

Detective Ellis gave the younger detective a skeptical look. "A bag taped over her head?"

"Yes, sir, a small bag taped around her neck as if she was suffocated, which is apparently what happened. She also appears to be bound. Her hands and feet have been duct taped." The younger detective approached the body and squatted.

A crime scene investigator was called over to cut the bag off the victim's head. As he did so, a hush fell over the crowd. Detective Ellis could feel the stare coming from the lady he had talked to as she stood with a jacket draped over her shoulders and her hands together by her mouth, praying.

Once the bag was removed from the victim's head, Detective Ellis stared at the lifeless form before him, unable to look up, knowing his eyes would betray him. "I know who she is." He shook his head as crime scene techs began snapping pictures at different angles. "She lived in this house. That's her mother standing right there in the yard."

He looked up and locked eyes with Yana's mother. She began to shake her head in disbelief. Ellis reluctantly walked over, broke the news to her, and watched her crumble to the ground, sobbing. Unable to look on any longer, he turned and walked off. The neighbors could tend to her. He had a murderer or murderers to catch, and while he didn't know who killed Yana, he had a good idea where to start looking.

Southside Mafia.

***

Shea was finally released from the hospital after three weeks of close care. Fresh air filled her lungs and sunshine touched her face as she smiled despite being permanently paralyzed from the waist down. A car was waiting at the curb, doors open as her mother wheeled her toward it in a wheelchair. She was lifted into the car by her step-father and driven home.

She heard about Yana's murder and watched the Channel 2 Action News segment about it. Just like everyone else in Riverdale, she heard Yana was murdered for snitching on Huncho and Flame. What no one knew was who was personally responsible for the murder. Her death brought no joy to Shea's heart, though. She would still be confined to a wheelchair for the rest of her life.

They pulled into their new home, a house down the street, also off Garden Walk. Shea became anxious. It felt like forever since she had been home. She was placed in her wheelchair and pushed toward the door where a ramp had already been installed just for her. In fact, her step-father made sure every part of the house was accessible to her by using his carpentry skills to make small ramps and place them wherever they needed to be for her to move throughout the house.

Her mother opened the door and stepped to the side, allowing her to be pushed by her step-father.

As soon as she came through the foyer, she was greeted by family and friends with a big "Welcome Home" banner displayed across the living room. "Surprise!" everyone yelled in unison.

All she could do was smile as tears filled her eyes.

Each of her family and friends came over, welcoming her home with hugs, gifts, and kisses on the cheek. Someone turned the music on and the welcome home get-together turned into a small party.

"I'm so glad to have you home," Brandi smiled, sitting in a chair next to Shea at the kitchen table. "I've already figured out how we're going to sneak you out the house, but we'll talk about that later."

"Y'all must know some magic, because it's going to be hell getting her out of here past me and her mother!" Shea's step-father said with a bit of humor. "That makes me think I better keep my gift I was going to give her."

"*Was* going to give to me?" Shea said. "What you mean, *was*? Where they do that at?"

Her step-father shrugged. "Well, you talking 'bout sneaking out on me, and the gift will only aid you."

"Mama, what he got for me?" Shea looked at her mother in all seriousness.

"I don't have anything to do with that. You know I don't get involved in y'all business." Her mother waived her off. "Remember when you was thirteen and he bought you that cell phone I didn't want you to have, and you told me to stop hating and stay out of y'all business? Well, I'm staying out of it."

The room erupted in laughter, and Shea smiled at the fond and distant memory. Her step-father got up and left the room while she and her mother went back and forth. He returned sitting in a motorized wheelchair with two gift bags hanging from each armrest. Shea smiled ear-to-ear. Inside the bags were an MP3 player, a new cell phone, perfume, and a necklace with a small diamond cross on it, along with several other things.

Her step-father lifted her up and put her in the new chair. Shea searched for the speedometer. "How fast it go?"

"Not fast enough to be in the street, you can bet that!" her mother said.

"I don't know about that, now!" one of her aunts said. "I done seen plenty of folks riding 'round downtown where I work at."

They continued to talk and laugh until sunset, and by nightfall Brandi, Meeka, and Zaria were leaving with promises to return the following day. They left and went over to Dre's spot where he and other Squad affiliates were hanging. Just as they were pulling up, Katrina, Tee, and Ericka were pulling off. Brandi and Meeka didn't notice them. Zaria didn't see them, either. All Brandi knew was it was a carload of females.

***

"Another teenager's body was found dead and is believed to be another victim of the Riverdale-originated Southside Mafia street gang!" the news reporter stated during her special report. "It's the fourth murder possibly linked to the infamous Southside Mafia. The two men in these pictures are Justin 'Flame' Howard and Daldrick 'Huncho' Blanding, who are top-ranking members of the gang. They are wanted for the murder of Deontae 'Taliban' Chambers, who is believed to have been an affiliate of Hit Squad Taliban, a rival gang that started in College Park and proliferated into the Clayton County area. Howard and Blanding are suspected to be involved with other murders, as well, and are...."

Detective Ellis sat in his living room watching the special report on Channel 2 Action News with his feet up on his coffee table and a beer in his hand. He stared at Huncho's mug shot with pure hatred as he remembered the interview he had with him during his hospital stay.

I didn't fall from heaven. I came up from hell. Understand me, Detective-Whatever-Your-Name-Is? And before I betray the life I live, I'd rather die or spend the rest of my life in jail!

Detective Ellis doubted he would ever forget those words, let alone the seriousness in which they were spoken. This was so true that even as he stared into Huncho's eyes on the television screen, the words could be heard clearly in his head as if he was seated on the couch with him. He knew Huncho was more than likely responsible for the murder of Yana, who had been his only witness and the only one who cooperated from within the Mafia. It sickened him that such an animal could still be out walking the streets.

The special report ended and he popped some peanuts in his mouth, grabbing another beer. Returning to the living room, he pulled his phone out and called the lead investigator of the Fugitive Task Force. A brief conversation later, he learned they had yet to find a lead. He thanked the investigator and asked to be kept up to date.

He flipped open his laptop, pulled up his case files, and went over his notes. Reading over the part about Huncho being shot, he thought about the encounter at the hospital with Dre and pulled up his information. He turned up the bottle as he stared at his mug shot and wiped his mouth after the contents had washed down his esophagus.

"Well, Mr. Chambers, I think it's time to pay you a visit."

***

Huncho bought a 1991 Brougham Chevy Caprice and had it painted pearl black. He put some 24-inch Ashanti rims on it and had the inside done with a butter-color ostrich material. He had the motor tricked out and a special transmission installed to withstand the powerful motor. On the trunk he had an airbrushed picture painted of the city on fire with the letters "SSM" in calligraphy. In the background of the painting there were ski-masked figures holding AK-47s.

When he first saw the work, he was unsatisfied. He felt it was missing something, so the artist added a few bullet holes in the trunk as if the car had been shot up and some smoke coming from the barrels of the AKs as if they had just been fired. Then he added empty shell casings at the bottom.

"Now that's what's up!" Huncho said when he returned to pick up the car.

After the incident in the parking lot of the club, they had no more problems from the locals when they showed face on the scene. A few people from around the way asked Gator what was up with them, and he gave them all the same answer. "They're from the outskirts of Atlanta. They got the work, and they strapped the fuck up!"

125

Elijah R. Freeman

They were down to one brick, and Gator had already put in an order for half of it. With the work nearly gone, they contemplated returning home to re-up. They both wanted to go back to Riverdale, but knew the risks and dangers of such a move. Flame's main concern was getting some money to his mother so she could retain him a lawyer. Huncho claimed the same intent, but was really missing home more than anything.

"So, what the move is, bra?" Huncho stepped from the bathroom and sat on the side of the bed. "It's your call. You know I don't really give a fuck."

Flame shrugged. "I don't know. We really need to find out how it's looking first, 'cause you know it might be on fire since that bitch Yana got found."

Huncho lay back on the bed, pondering the situation. "Yeah, you right about that."

Flame's phone rang. Checking the screen to find it was Tip, he ignored the call.

After about thirty minutes of going back and forth and a couple phone calls, they both agreed to go back home for a few days once the work was gone. Their plan was to cop some work, deliver the money for the lawyers, knock Dre off, then head back to Alabama.

Three days later they were on I-20 west headed back to Riverdale in separate cars with Monica and Tip. They arrived in Georgia at 3:30 in the morning. They got off on Exit 41, turning onto Bullsboro Drive in Newnan and got a room at the Motel 8 down the strip in Tip's name. They were awaiting a certain call before stepping foot back in Clayton County. The females were eager to head out and visit the hot spots of Atlanta, but Huncho and Flame told them all that would come in due time. That didn't stop them from nagging them about it as soon as the sun came up, though.

"Look, shawdy, we came here for business, not pleasure or no fucking vacation," Huncho told Monica.
126

"But what we gonna do is let you and Tip go out by yourselves so y'all can get y'all party on. While y'all doing that, me and my bra gon' handle business."

She seemed agreeable to the suggestion and showed her appreciation by pulling his dick out and sticking it in her mouth. After about an hour of sex, he hopped in the shower, anxiously awaiting sunset. He sent Monica out for food, and while she and Tip were gone, Flame joined him in the room.

"I'm gon' get that money to my mama tonight." Flame sat at the small table in the room rolling a blunt. "I holla'd at Katrina, too. Nothing been going on but the news."

"She know we back in town?" Huncho flicked through channels.

"Naw, I ain't tell her all that. I just told her to stay on point until I call her because I'm going to need her to handle some shit for me."

Later that night the girls went out, whipping the Chrysler 300. They wouldn't have a hard time getting around. They already knew how to get to the expressway. All they had to do was get on I-20 east and ride until they got to downtown Atlanta, where finding a club would be a walk in the park.

Huncho and Flame left a couple hours after them to meet up with Katrina and give her the lawyer fare to deliver to Flame's mother. After that and a short reunion they went their separate ways. Huncho ended up going to see Camry to give her some dick and some more money.

At 5:43 that morning they set out to meet with Purp, Huncho's coke plug. He wasn't the type to boast, brag, or flex about what he had like so many of the others he had run across. The only time they kicked it was on some business-type shit. Purp was the founder of the Benji Family, an organization that started in Youngstown, Ohio

127

and spread throughout a couple of states. They were known in the music industry and had a chain of clubs they owned and ran. In the streets, though, they were known for the work they supplied and their stack-or-starve attitude.

Huncho contacted him and told him of his situation, and being the solid nigga he was, he extended his hand to help in what way he could without jeopardizing his own freedom and family. He knew Huncho was on the run and in need of some serious cash, so when Huncho called, he answered. They met up in a Burlington Coat Factory parking lot in Morrow on Mt. Zion Boulevard

"Long time, no see, G." Purp gave Huncho a handshake-hug. "Why you just now using my number, though? We could've done some big things out here in these streets, man."

"Man, I already know, but you know how shit is. Nigga get out here and get caught up in all type of shit," Huncho said. "And, to be honest, I didn't even think you was doing it this big out here."

Purp laughed him off. "Yo, aye, dude. I'm gonna let ya be on your way 'cause this ain't the time or place to be kicking it, feel me?" Purp looked over at the black Excursion with dark-tinted windows that he got out of and jerked his head upward. Two females got out of the back, both carrying big duffle bags and walked over to Huncho's car where Flame sat inside, waiting. They put the bags in the car and strutted back to the truck. Once insidem they checked the brown paper bag with the money Flame just gave them. Everything straight, they let the window down halfway and gave Purp a nod.

"A'ight, G. Be careful." Purp dapped Huncho up, then he hopped in the passenger side of the black Excursion and pulled off.

"That nigga riding with that much work with some hos. He must don't think he can get got or something," Flame said once Huncho was back in the car.

Triggadale

"That's my folk, bra. And it ain't no telling who else was in that truck or out here with him. He ain't slippin like that, shawdy." Huncho said.

Just as the words left his mouth two cars jumped behind Purp's Excursion and another pulled up in front of him.

When they got back to the room and opened the bags, Huncho smiled from ear to ear. In one of the duffle bags was an extra brick.

Elijah R. Freeman

Chapter 13

Huncho and Flame sent Monica and Tip back with the work and were waiting patiently on the call from Katrina. She was with Dre. The Queens had been with him and the Squad all day long. They had infiltrated Hit Squad Taliban and gained their trust, sometimes even spending the night with Dre and his crew. She was fucking Dre, but her feelings weren't involved. In the past she'd sucked and fucked several guys for the Mafia, most of them for robberies. It was all the same to her. If someone wasn't Mafia, she didn't give a damn about them.

The house was the same as usual: a bunch of Squad affiliates hanging around drinking, smoking, and talking shit. She and Dre were on the porch with Mario, Southside, Trav, and Waka. Also on the porch was Tee, Daja, and Ericka, who had been accompanying her on the mission at hand. They were laughing and kicking it, two blunts floating around in rotation. Katrina was up under Dre as if they were seriously in love. He leaned against the patio rail and she leaned back against him, her soft ass pressing against his hard dick.

"Shawdy, how long you gon' be out tonight?" Dre asked Katrina.

She ground her hips subtly. "How long you want me to be out, daddy?"

"Until you put me to sleep again," he whispered in her ear before kissing her neck.

Gotti grabbed Tee, who he'd taken to dicking down on a regular. "You stayin', too?"

"If you want me to, I will."

"Shid, what type of answer that is?" Gotti gripped Tee's ripe booty. "Shawdy, you know I want you to stay."

An hour later Daja and Ericka prepared to leave. Katrina asked Dre to ride with her to drop the girls off, and he obliged. Gotti and Tee decided to go as well. To Dre and Gotti it all seemed random. Little did they know the axe had fallen.

They piled into Katrina's tan Buick Century. Dre sat in the passenger seat and everyone else sat in the back, Tee on Gotti's lap. They arrived on Brown Road off S.R. 54 thirty minutes later, pulling curbside in front of a random house. Street lights lined the road filled with modern-style homes, and the neighborhood seemed fairly quiet.

Dre was laid back, high with his eyes closed, oblivious to Huncho creeping up on the car with a 12-gauge – ironically, the same weapon used to end his brother's life. Katrina popped the locks, arousing Dre from his slumber.

"Get the fuck out the car, nigga!" Huncho snatched the door open. Gotti couldn't move fast enough with Tee sitting on his lap as Flame snatched open his door and put a P90 Ruger to his head.

Dre got out of the car slowly with his hands raised as Huncho aimed the pump at his midsection. His Glock 40 peeked out of the top of his front pocket, but he knew if he went for it he would be shot. Staring at Huncho caused him to smell his own blood as it pumped through his veins. He sobered up quickly, knowing he had been caught slipping.

Tee slid off Gotti's lap and he got out of the car, complying, then all at once he lunged at Flame, who fired off a couple of shots into his torso. The shots stole Huncho's attention, giving Dre the split second to go for his pistol. Tee hopped back in the car and Katrina smashed out.

The slugs connected with Gotti's vest, and it felt as though his ribs were being hit with a baseball bat, knocking the wind from him, but he rushed on with the force of Ray Lewis going for a quarterback, tackling Flame to the ground. It was a life or death situation, and he was going all out, thriving off of pure adrenaline.

Huncho and Dre stood aiming their tools at each other. Huncho knew he had a better chance with the pump and vest he had on, except Dre wasn't aiming at his body. He was aiming at his head. They stood in silence as if the world stopped spinning, looking into each other's eyes.

Huncho saw the same look he had the night Dre shot him, and Dre was looking into the eyes of the one responsible for his brother's death. Two more gunshots came from where Flame and Gotti wrestled on the ground, but neither of them dared to look, knowing the glance would be a fatal mistake for whoever chose to do so first.

A Clayton County squad car skidded to a stop and two officers jumped out, brandishing pistols. Someone must've called them after hearing gunfire. Flame, who had shot Gotti in the neck and face, pushed his dead body off, hopped up, and opened fire. The officers took cover behind the driver and passenger door and returned fire.

"What we gonna do, shawdy?" Huncho yelled above the gunfire, pump trained on Dre. "We just gon' let these muthafuckin' crackas kill us?"

Flame was walking toward the police, both pistols spitting.

Dre bit down on his bottom lip, breathing heavily through his nose with a tight grip on his Glock, still trained on Huncho. "You killed my brother!"

"So we gon' let these crackas kill us!"

Flame ran out of bullets and went to take cover, but the police seized the opportunity and opened fire, dropping Flame instantly. Huncho and Dre turned their weapons on the law, simultaneously letting loose as they backed away.

More police flooded the scene, and they both fled into the woods, neither having the ammunition left to continue shooting. The backup opened fire on them and Dre was hit in the leg, but continued to run as best as he could.

133

Huncho's long legs made him run like a deer into the dark woods until he eventually fell in a creek. He was about to get out and start running again until he saw the spotlight of a helicopter.

He knew from previous experience that the helicopter had a heat sensor on it, so his best bet was to stay in the cold water. The creek was a little over knee deep. Thinking fast, he crouched low and began crawling down the stream quietly, but as quickly as possible. Every now and then when the helicopter got too close he submerged himself to let the water cool him off. Eventually the sound of propellers faded behind him.

***

Katrina, Tee, Bria, and Daja saw all the police shooting past them as they turned onto Webb Road by Pointe South Middle Elementary School. They knew Flame shot Gotti when he charged him, but with all the police they were seeing, they knew something more major was going on.

Katrina pulled her phone from her case, quickly located Flame's number, and pressed talk, but after several rings all she got was his voicemail. She sent him a quick text telling him a bunch of police were coming their way and to call her back. She sent Huncho the same message. When she turned on Lake Ridge Parkway, more police cruisers flew past her, racing down Highway 85, lights flashing and sirens blaring.

"Girl, something ain't right." Daja sat in the passenger seat, nervous. "What all these police doing out here?"

"I don't know. I wish one of them would call me back and let me know they're alright, at least," Katrina said.

They all went home and waited for the call that never came. Katrina continued to try both of their numbers, but never got an answer or response to her text messages. She put her phone on the charger and laid it by her head. Then she dozed off to sleep.

She woke up the next morning to her phone ringing and answered on the third ring without bothering to see who it was. "Hello?"

"Girl, turn to the news." It was Daja. "Hurry up!"

Katrina fished for her remote under the covers. She found it and turned her television to Channel 2 Action News. They were reporting live from Brown Road with the words *Three dead after police shootout* scrolling across the screen. Flame, Gotti, and Dre's picture were being shown, and a larger picture of Huncho was under the heading *Murder Suspect and Fugitive*. His real name was under the picture.

"He is believe to be the fourth person who was at the scene, but somehow managed to avoid capture and escaped after a lengthy shootout with law enforcement officials." The reporter went on to tell Huncho's history.

Dre had been found dead in the woods after he bled to death from the shot in his leg. The bullet hit a major artery. Huncho managed to escape four miles downstream, leaving the K-9 unit with no scent to pick up. It had been determined Flame shot the two officers who had been wounded during the shootout. What everyone, including Katrina, was wondering now was one thing: Where was Huncho?

***

After an interview with Channel 5 News covered a story on Huncho, who made Georgia's Most Wanted list, Detective Ellis went straight to the headquarters. It had been determined Huncho was at the scene of the shootout by the fingerprints lifted from the shotgun left behind and the car found parked down the street, which had his fingerprints as well.

Detective Ellis was amazed by his boldness once he saw the car's paint job. It was as if Huncho was taunting him and the entire law enforcement with the airbrushed pictures on the Chevy. He was also irritated that Huncho always seem to thwart his attempts to gain a lead. Now, finally, he had made one mistake that may just cost him everything.

The license plate on the Chevy had just taken the search to Alabama.

***

"Please, mister, don't hurt me!" the elderly white woman begged as Huncho dragged her into her house with a .45 to her head and an arm around her neck. "My purse is in the back. You can have it!"

"Shut the fuck up! Don't say shit else!" he said through clenched teeth.

Huncho had made it all the way to Fayetteville and stayed in a barn for a day and a half before emerging, making sure he had gotten away. His phone didn't work due to it getting wet when he was in the creek. All he had was the money in his pocket and the .45, which was his backup pistol.

The old lady had heard her dog barking as she lay on the couch after putting in her morning load of laundry. Thinking it was some type of scavenger in her trash can out back that had her dogs barking, she grabbed a broom and went to take a look. As soon as she opened the door, Huncho raised the pistol to her face and snatched her in a weaver. He knew she was home alone from watching her while he was in her barn. Once he was in the house, he tied the lady up and gagged her.

Triggadale

Being that he went without food and water for nearly two days, he was famished. The first thing he did after tying the lady up was go straight to the kitchen. He felt weak and knew he had to eat before he went any further. After cooking and devouring a little breakfast, he sat and contemplated his next move. He knew he had to leave town immediately, but as he watched the news, he realized there was something else he needed to do.

Change his appearance.

So, after eating another plate, he got straight to the task. Dreads clipped, he returned to the old lady and put the pistol to her head, demanding the keys to her Lincoln Town car. She nodded in the direction of her purse and he snatched it from her bedpost. He grabbed her keys and cell phone and waited until nightfall to set back out to Alabama.

As he drove, he thought about Flame and the five bricks they had sent back to Alabama. His heart ached for his fallen comrade. With all that was going on he hadn't been able to mourn him, but as he drove tears glided down his cheeks. He didn't even notice until he glanced in his rearview mirror and the early morning sun gleamed off the salty stream. He was stunned, like a healthy man who learned suddenly he had a terminal illness. At one point all hope fled from him, but he knew Flame wouldn't want that. He had to remain ten toes down. Remembering this, he wiped his face and applied pressure to the gas pedal as he continued to ponder the loss of his right hand. He shook his head solemnly.

Flame would always be his brother. No one could take his place. It killed him that he had to leave him on the scene, but there was nothing he could do for him. He was already dead. The best thing he could do for him was survive. He had to go on. The Mafia had to go on.

He was off schedule. The more he thought about the situation, the faster he drove, but he quickly checked himself. The last thing he needed was to be stopped for speeding.

Then, like a sledgehammer to the face, an idea hit him. He pulled out the cell phone he had taken from the old lady and dialed his own number. When the voicemail came on, he punched in the code to gain access. Going through all of his messages, which were mostly from Katrina, he located the one he was looking for and listened for the number the automated voice said the message had come from.

Moving quickly, he punched in the numbers and locked it in. After going through the rest of the messages, he called the number. The first time he called he got no answer, so he called right back, and the person picked up on the second ring.

"Hello?"

"Monica?"

"Yeah, who this?"

"What's up, it's ya boy. Everything good on yo' end, ain't it?"

"Yeah, baby, everything straight. Where you at?" she asked. "And why you not here yet? I thought y'all was coming right behind us?"

He felt a little relieved hearing they had made it back safe with the work, and Huncho relaxed somewhat. "My partner got knocked."

"Who, Flame?"

"Hell yeah. I been tryna get him out," he lied. "But shid, I'm headed your way now. I should be there in a couple hours, a'ight? So just hold that down for me 'til I get there."

"Okay, baby, you know I got you." After a few more short words, they ended the call.

Huncho got on the expressway and set the cruise control on sixty to make sure he wasn't speeding. He was fiending for a cigarette, but there was no way he was stopping at a store until he crossed the state line. With that thought, he looked at the dash to check the gas meter and saw he had nearly a full tank.

When I get down there, I'ma get off two of them bricks and head to New Orleans, he thought, reclining his seat. *I know the money gone that we left in Newnan, but fuck it. It is what it is.*

***

At that same moment, the neighbor of the elderly lady he left tied up was beating on her door. She had called several times before coming and was now worried because she had yet to answer, and that was unusual for her in the morning. When she walked around to the bedroom window, she saw her friend of twenty years bound and gagged, lying facedown on the floor.

***

Katrina had just gotten out of the shower and was putting lotion on her body, listening to a Mafioso named P-nut's new song *You'll Never Understand.* She had one foot on the bed, lotioning her leg as she sang along with the music.

She stood up with nothing but a thong on and began grinding her body seductively to the music as she watched herself in the mirror. She told herself over and over she was going to be a Stroker's dancer, but never built up the nerve to go audition. She knew without a doubt she had the body and the moves because she had danced at Mafia get-togethers on several different occasions and was always the best out of the girls who danced with her.

At 5'1" with a small waist, thick thighs, and a perfect round ass to go with her flat stomach and perfect breasts, she was definitely a bad bitch. Her cute, innocent face,

139

perfect smile, and bedroom eyes that were naturally hazel only enhanced her beauty, giving her model quality.

She slowly rubbed her body as she gyrated her hips, staring into the mirror. She studied her facial expressions and smiled, biting down on her bottom lip before climbing onto her bed to stand in the middle and watch herself grind sexually to the rhythm of the music. As she stood on the bed, she began to rub her hands all over her body sensually, allowing them to slide down to the part that made her a woman. Once her hands touched, she spread the folds to see the pinkness in the mirror.

A knock at the door snapped her from her trance and she hopped off the bed, embarrassed.

"Yes!" she yelled over the music after hearing her mother call her name. "One minute, I'm getting dressed."

"It's somebody out here to see you, and you need to get out here!" her mother yelled.

"I'm coming, Mama!" She slipped into some boy shorts and a tank top, making her look even sexier. She stepped out of her bedroom and walked down the hall to the living room where she heard her mother's voice.

When she stepped into the living room, she froze in her tracks at the sight of two detectives. Ellis and Foster. She remembered them from questioning when Yana shot Shea. More importantly, she remembered the things, as well as the people, they questioned her about. So to see them in her living room after what happened last night, she knew it couldn't be good, and it showed in her face.

"Katrina, you might want to get dressed," Ellis said. "We need to take you in for questioning."

Katrina was visibly shaken. "Questioning about what? I haven't done anything wrong."

"Baby, just put on some clothes," her mother said. "I'm going, too. I'll be waiting in the front."

After she was dressed and came out of the room, she was led out of the house and driven to Clayton County

Police Headquarters. When they arrived, she was placed in an interrogation room and Detective Ellis wasted no time.

"Katrina, where were you last night?" There was seriousness in his voice that made her nervous.

"With my friends Daja, Tee, and Alicia."

"And just where were y'all exactly? Give me a location."

She knew not to say Dre's name. "At Alicia's boyfriend's house in Forest Park."

He switched up his line of questioning "Do you know Deandre Chambers, otherwise known as Dre?"

"No, I don't think so," she lied.

"When was the last time you saw Blanding or Howard?"

"Who?"

"'Huncho' or 'Flame.'" Ellis emphasized his words by making quotation mark gestures.

She shifted in her seat and began to fidget. "It's been a long time. I would say right before they went on the run."

"So you haven't talked to or heard from them, either?"

"No, I haven't," she lied for the fifth time in five minutes.

Ellis opened a folder and leafed through some papers until he found what he was looking for, then he slid the paper across the table to her. "Now, Katrina, we're going to try this again and see if you're ready to tell the truth, because last night you texted them both and told them the police were heading their way at the same time they were in a shootout with law enforcement."

As Katrina stared down at the document containing her cell phone history, Ellis pointed and continued. "And right here are several calls you made to Dre's phone, and I have a lot more to show you to prove you're lying, Katrina. Your boy Howard's phone was found at the scene, and there was a text in there from your phone that said you had Dre and his friend in the car with you. Katrina?"

141

Katrina looked up as tears welled up in her eyes and spilled over her cheeks.

"Now they're both dead."

Chapter 14

Huncho was back in Alabama and staying at Monica's house with her and her two kids. He moved all his things from the hotel room to her house and was using her to move the work. He no longer dealt with just Gator, like he and Flame had started out doing. He was supplying the city in an attempt to get off the work as quickly as possible so he could relocate. He felt he was too close to Georgia in Alabama.

Gator didn't like what he was doing with the work because it was cutting into his pockets, but he couldn't complain because he was still getting the best prices in the city. Being that he was the man in the city and he knew his hood and city like the back of his hand, he noticed a change since Huncho had returned. He began to hang back, only dealing with a select few due to what he was seeing in and around the city. With everybody hustling and getting money from the work Huncho was basically giving away, it seemed like he was the only one noticing what was going on. Being the smart hustler he was, he fell back from the game so he'd be free to hustle another day.

Gator answered his phone as he sat in his living room watching ESPN. "What it do, mane?"

"Shid, tryna fuck witcha on a li'l come-up," one of his customers named Nate replied. "You on deck?"

"Naw, homeboy. I believe them feds in town, so I'm laying low, ya dig?"

"Damn, first Charlie Black, now you! He was saying the same thing about how he think them folks finna hit. You think it's ya boys from Riverdale they're after?"

"Could be," Gator said. "It's been a lot of work since they showed up, and them niggas just popped up out of nowhere. My guess is the feds was probably on them 'round their way, so they ran down here and set up shop."

"Yeah, that sound 'bout right, but let me hit you back. I got some folks on hold, and I ain't tryna miss no money, feel me?"

Gator hung up, thinking about his sister Monica. He knew Huncho moved in with her and she was helping him hustle the work off. Now, with the feds in town, he felt he needed to warn her to fall back before she ended up indicted. If Nate said Charlie Black mentioned something about the feds lurking, then nine times out of ten that's what it was.

He looked at the time on his phone and got up off his sofa, headed to the door. "Baby, I'm finna run over to my sister house for a minute!" he yelled back to his girlfriend as he walked out of the door.

***

Detective Ellis rushed over to Edna Miller's home when he received the information about the invasion she was the victim of. It wasn't just the invasion that led him to the victim's home, it was the description of the person responsible that grasped his attention. Hearing it could be the one he was looking for, he was off racing.

Edna's neighbor Josephine had become suspicious when she hadn't answered her phone or come over for their daily game of scrabble and a cup of tea. She found her bound and gagged facedown on the floor after looking through her bedroom window and ran as fast as she could back to her house to call the police. She didn't know if her friend was dead or alive as she ran back to her house, nearly passing out in her husband's arms from fear and shortness of breath when she made it through her front door.

Triggadale

On his way to the crime scene, Detective Ellis was updated on the details of the incident. When he heard the suspect cut his hair in the victim's house and left what appeared to be a dreadlock by the bathroom sink, Ellis sped up, feeling a hundred percent sure it was Huncho. That in mind, he put an APB out on the victim's car.

When Ellis arrived at the scene, there were two ambulances, a fire truck, several policemen and investigators, and a perimeter of yellow crime scene tape. He parked as close as he could to the scene among the other dispatched help in the rural neighborhood, walking toward the house and ducking under the tape.

"I believe it was him," Foster said. He had made it to the scene not too long ago himself.

"What makes you so sure?" Ellis asked.

"The description she gave and the dreadlock with the dyed tip that he probably accidentally dropped after cutting his hair. And after searching her barn, it looks like he camped out in there for a day or two."

Ellis went in and questioned Edna, who lay across her bed with an oxygen mask strapped to her face. After a quick questioning and showing a photo of Huncho that she positively identified, Detective Ellis was on the phone with the Georgia Bureau of Investigation agent who had been involved with the case since Huncho made the Georgia's most wanted list. Ellis read off a list of details he gathered from the victim and investigators in Fayetteville.

"He also took her cell phone." He gave the GBI agent the victim's number.

Leaving the scene, Ellis felt like he was closing in on Huncho, and it wouldn't be long before he was slapping handcuffs on his wrists.

Two days later the victim's car was found in Livingston, Alabama in a Walmart parking lot. It had been free of prints, but after checking the parking lot

145

surveillance camera footage, it showed Huncho getting out of the car, walking across the parking lot, and hopping in the passenger seat of a Nissan Maxima, instantly making Alabama the focal point of their search. What put the icing on the cake was Edna's phone record. Three calls were made to a Monica Williams. After discovering she was a Sumter County resident, they deduced she was more than likely the female who had picked him up in the parking lot, according to the time of the calls and the time showing on the surveillance footage.

The interview with Katrina and her friends had been very helpful to the investigation. With their cooperation he had been able to secure seventeen warrants for Southside Mafia affiliates they had been wanting. Once the pressure was on, several of them began cooperating with the investigation as well. Many of them even pointed the finger at Huncho, realizing they were facing prison time themselves. The investigation had finally picked up, but no Huncho.

It was too soon to celebrate, but Ellis remained adamant. He had never been this close before. Then again, Huncho had never made this many mistakes.

It was almost like he wanted to be found.

***

Huncho, Monica, and her kids had decided to go out to eat at a soul food restaurant in Scooba, Mississippi called La Wendy's Diner. Monica had been suspicious of Huncho since his return. It started when she picked him up nearly 35 miles away from her home and he got in with an uneven haircut. Then when they jumped on the expressway, he slung his phone, or so she believed, out of the window and told her to do the same with hers. He bought her a new one the same day, but it was still a red flag. Not to mention his clothes smelled of mildew and his shoes were muddy. She

146

instantly disbelieved his story about the reason Flame hadn't come back with him and how he had been held up trying to get him out, but couldn't.

Her next alert had come when Gator warned her about the feds being in town and possibly looking for Huncho. If that didn't open her eyes, later that day when she and Huncho were riding and the police got behind them, Huncho grabbed his pistol and cocked it. She knew then that something was amiss.

"Y'all ready, shawdy?"

She nodded. Huncho wiped his hands on a napkin, pulled money from his pocket, and called a waitress over.

"Did y'all enjoy y'all meal?" the waitress asked with a smile.

"Yes, it was fine," Monica said.

Meal paid for, they left the restaurant and loaded up in the car. Huncho rocked a low fade and wore a pair of Cartier glasses and a simple metal bead chain with two dog tags hanging from it that had small diamonds going around the edge.

The bulletproof vest he wore made him seem a little more buff than he was, so the agents in the parking lot and the Fugitive Task Force weren't quite sure if it was him until they ran the license plate of the car and Monica's name came up, matching the person he called from Edna's cell phone.

They pulled out of the restaurant parking lot with Monica driving. Huncho watched the side view mirror out of habit to see if he was being followed. He watched on and off for about ten minutes into the ride and was satisfied they weren't being tailed. He didn't realized he was being followed because the tail continued to switch to prevent him from seeing the same car one too many times.

After dropping the kids off at Monica's mother's house, they headed straight home as the sun began to set. Fives minutes later the power went out, and five seconds after that the front door was rammed off the hinges.

Huncho was in the bathroom when he heard the noise, followed by Monica's screams. His first thought was a drug bust because Monica had warned him about the feds being in town. He wasn't worried about any work being found because they had it stashed in a storage place. Plus he had a fake ID he had paid $2,500 for that was made by some Hispanics. So, as no work was in the house, he would be cool.

Then he thought about the Glock .45 in his back pocket and bulletproof vest he was clearly wearing with no shirt to cover it, along with all the other guns in the house.

"Fuck!"

He ran to take a peep out the window. Unmarked Crown Vics, F-150s, Dodge Chargers, and Sumter County Police squad cars were in the yard and lining the streets. He could hear the sound of helicopters as well. He opened the bathroom closet and snatched a Glock .40 from the top shelf. Every room had a gun in it he could quickly grab, but he wished like hell he was in the bedroom where the real firepower was.

He cracked the bathroom door and saw a figure in full tactical gear stepping around the corner in a squatting position with an MP5 aimed in front of him. He snatched the door open and began firing at the figure with both pistols as he stepped from the bathroom, spitting fire as he back-stepped toward the bedroom where he could hear Monica's screams coming from.

The figure he was shooting at returned fire as the slugs hit his Kevlar vest, knocking him back against the wall, causing his fellow SWAT Team officers to drag him to safety. Some shot blindly up the hall for cover as they dragged the officer to safety, but Huncho had already entered the bedroom.

Quickly, he flipped the mattress and grabbed the AK-47 with an extra hundred-round drum as Monica continued to scream in the corner where she had balled up in a fetal position. Moving faster now, he opened up the nightstand drawer and pulled out a Ruger 9mm and tucked it on his waistline.

Hearing the squeaks from the hallway floor as the SWAT Team advanced up the hall toward him, he snatched the door open with the choppa held at waist level, squeezing the trigger and knocking SWAT Team officers back down the hall as others tripped and fell over themselves trying to escape the fire.

"You want it, muthafucka? Come get it," he yelled as he walked over a fallen SWAT officer, putting a bullet in his head.

Shots began coming through the windows from all angles, but he stood his ground in the hallway and continued to hold the SWAT Team off by letting off steady rounds. Monica managed to crawl out of the bedroom as slugs and wood splinters flew over her head, only to be snatched up by Huncho and used as a human shield as he slowly made his way down the hall.

"Y'all back the fuck up or this bitch dying!" He held Monica in a yoke with the choppa still pressed at his hip, aimed down the hall.

"He's got a hostage!" a SWAT Team officer shouted after peeping around the corner. "Cease fire! I repeat, hold your fire!"

The other SWAT officers began yelling the command into the mouthpiece attached to their helmets, and they began to retreat out the front door, seeing that it had turned into a hostage situation.

"That's right, muthafuckas, you better tell 'em!" Huncho yelled as he continued down the hall.

***

Because Huncho had crossed state lines, agents from the Georgia Bureau of Investigation had been sent to assist in his arrest. When calls went out that he had fired on Sumter County SWAT officers and the situation turned into a standoff with three officers possibly dead and an involuntary captive, local news stations in Georgia and Alabama flocked to the scene.

Ellis was unable to let go of what he proclaimed *his* investigation. He called an old Navy buddy who owned a small aircraft. He and Foster wanted to get to Alabama quick, fast, and in a hurry.

***

Back in Riverdale, Camry had been flicking through channels when she stopped at the CNN breaking news story. The bottom of the screen read "STANDOFF — HOSTAGE SITUATION." Then Huncho's picture appeared in the upper left-hand corner. The reporter was giving a live account of what was taking pace as well as what led up to the situation.

Camry began to cry at the mention of the three dead officers from the SWAT Team. She knew Huncho would never be a part of her baby's life now. She began to think about all the times they shared, and as she stared at the television screen, memories began to flood her mind. He wasn't who they thought he was. He wasn't who he thought he was. Not to her, he wasn't. He was so much more.

Her mother walked in her room at the sound of her sobs, about to ask what was wrong until she glanced at the television. Instantly she knew. She took her daughter into her embrace and began stroking her hair with compassion and understanding as they continued to watch the news in silence.

150

Chapter 15

At the Clayton County Detention Center, Mafiosos on all floors stood posted in front of the television, watching the special news report. Some of them wished they went out the same way. The ones who snitched felt like bitches on the inside. Those who knew Huncho personally knew he wasn't going out bad and would die for the Mafia, unlike those who turned state under pressure and went out like pussies. They knew Huncho lived for the Mafia and loved it like no other through the good, bad, and ugly, freedom or prison. So, as they stood under the televisions, looking up at the screens, they felt a sense of pride knowing they had thugged with him.

The televisions went off, signaling lockdown time, and on every floor of the jail Mafioso's broke out in fights and began to buck on the officers.

***

"Huncho, why are you doing this?" Monica cried. "Please, let me go. Don't hurt me. I got to raise my kids."

"If I have to tell you to shut the fuck up again, I'ma blow ya muthafuckin' head off!" he yelled in pure rage. "Now, bitch, shut up!"

Huncho paced back and forth in the windowless hallway, clutching the 9mm in his hand. The SWAT Team had no idea what part of the house he was in, so they remained neutral and didn't attempt to storm the house and risk the hostage's life. He could hear everything going on through the radio he had removed from one of the dead SWAT Team officers, so they couldn't sneak up on him.

The sun set and the house was absolutely silent due to the power being out. They had been in the house for over two hours now, and Monica was beginning to wear down from constantly crying. Several attempts had been made at negotiation, but Huncho refused all offers being that none had been in his favor. They had asked that the hostage be released several times, but he knew she was the only thing holding them off.

He made a call to Camry, and even to his mother, who to his surprise broke down in sobs, telling him how sorry she was for the lost times and for failing him as a mother. Genuine? He wasn't sure, but he told her he loved her and forgave her anyway. Camry tried to talk him into turning himself in, and that's when he told her he loved her, kiss his unborn child for him, and then ended the call.

He heard a familiar voice calling his name over a megaphone. He didn't answer until a phone number was yelled out for him to call. When he called, Detective Ellis answered on the first ring.

"Look, Blanding, it's over. You might as well give it up and come out of this mess with at least your life! You have no win. It's about 50 to 75 guns aimed at you right now, so let the girl go and come out with your hands locked behind your head. The entire nation is watching right now, so no one is going to hurt you, Blanding. Do you understand?"

Huncho chuckled a tired laugh. Pulling the Newport from his ear, he fired it up and took a pull, blowing out the smoke. "I see you still on that bullshit, huh? Don't you realize by now that I'm not one of them pussy-niggas you broke? My nigga, I don't even bend, so you'll never break me, ya understand? And this shit ain't over 'til I say it's over with!"

"Blanding, you're coming out of that house walking or in a goddamn body bag. It's up to you, son, and time is running out for you!" Ellis yelled.

"Oh yeah? I tell you what, then." Huncho took another pull from the Newport. Exhaling slowly, he took a deep breath. "If you come in and escort me out to make sure I'm safe, I'll give up. But that's the only way."

"That can be worked out. I'm going to stay on the phone with you as I come to you, alright?"

Foster and the police chief shot him disapproving gazes, which he ignored. In his mind Huncho was in a catch-22, which meant the opposite set of circumstances for himself. Win-Win.

Huncho's voice brought him back from his introspective thoughts. "That's what's up, but if they shoot, the girl will be in front of me when I open the door."

He put the Newport out and grabbed the AK leaning up against the wall next to him. He led Monica to the door and cracked it, listening to Ellis calmly talk to him as he approached the house. He waited until Ellis was at the bottom of the porch steps, then let Monica run out of the door. Ellis stopped until she was safe with the officers behind the squad cars.

"That was a good thing you just did, Blanding," Ellis said into the phone. "Now, I want you to step out the door with your hands raised."

Huncho stepped halfway out of the door with his left hand on his head, and then all at once he revealed the right side of his body that held the choppa and opened fire on Ellis, knocking him off his feet. "Fuck-nigga! I told you!"

He continued firing on the law enforcement officials, waiving the choppa side-to-side, spraying the barricade of squad cars as he walked toward them. He wore an arrogant smirk on his face as he held the AK in place and it spit out shells. His mind was made up that it was over with, and he was going out like a true Mafioso.

A bullet hit him in his shoulder and jerked him around, but he continued to let off round after round. Another slug hit him in the chest, knocking him back, but the Teflon vest was not penetrated. Pain shot through his body, but he pressed forward like a soldier drenched in blood and sweat, but never tears.

Elijah R. Freeman

As the gunfire echoed through the night, it sounded like a war zone. The bright spotlight from the helicopter shone down on him, giving the air sniper a clear shot as he lined Huncho's head up with the center of the scope's crosshairs.

With one squeeze of the trigger on the AR-15, it was over. Huncho's brains flew from the side of his head and he fell to the ground.

To the live viewers around the nation, it all seemed to happen in slow motion just before the news station killed the camera due to the gruesome scene. Over fifty local and SWAT Team officers began to inch toward him as others ran toward the house. Ellis lay dead at the bottom of the porch steps, and three SWAT Team officers lay dead inside.

Detective Foster ran over to Huncho and stopped to watch as the first officer approached and squatted over him, snatching the dog tags from around his neck and read them. One read 7-6, the other read 7-5. When the officer flipped them over and read the back, the message was clear reading from left to right.

Mafia Made.

Chapter 16

Boom! Boom! Boom!

A C.O. kicked his door.

In his cot, Huncho sat straight up from a dream and looked around the cell at bare walls. He was covered in sweat that dripped from his forehead.

"Get up, Blanding! You got court. I'll be back in ten minutes," Officer Cheeseboro said.

Huncho hopped up off his cot, went over to the sink, and dashed water in his face, looking in the metal mirror with a smile.

Three years ago he was sentenced to life plus five years for the murder of Taliban. After making it off the scene of the police shootout that had claimed Flame's life, he had been discovered passed out from hunger and exhaustion in Edna Miller's barn by Edna herself the following morning when she entered in search of a garden tool. Startled, she called the police immediately, and when he woke up he was handcuffed to the hospital bed. It was over with, or so everyone thought.

His mother took the money he gave her and got him a good lawyer. Then, through a Mafioso who was getting out of the County, he got word to the streets and sent the Mafia to get the bricks, money, and whatever was left of the work from Monica in Emelle, Alabama, who turned out to be too smart for her own good. She had paid the price with her life, as well as Gator, who was with her when they caught up with her.

With Yana dead, her testimony was still able to be used, but Huncho's lawyer discredited it by tainting her credibility with the probability of her confession being coerced due to the situation she had found herself in. In other words, she made it up to free herself.

As for the death of Tevo and the shootout with the police, there were no witnesses, and being that it had been night, police officers hadn't gotten a good look at him and had picked someone else in the line-up. All they knew was the suspect had dreads. The indictment for the murder of Tevo and Yana never made it past the grand jury. Huncho's lawyer had displayed an outstanding ability to create reasonable doubt. Still, he was convicted.

Immediately, Huncho's lawyer filed an appeal on the grounds of him being convicted off of circumstantial evidence, along with a few other trial errors he had found in his transcript. It had taken some time and all, but after filing the right motions, his new trial date was set. He was going back to Clayton County.

Brushing his teeth and getting dressed, he sat on the bed and waited for Cheeseboro to return.

He stepped in front of the cell door. "You ready?"

Huncho slowly rose from the bed and walked over to the cell door. He knew he was blessed with a second chance at life, unlike so many others.

He stayed true to what he believed in to the very end when others wavered and fell to the wayside. It hurt him to know niggas who had screamed Southside Mafia had turned state's witness when shit hit the fan. One thing was for sure, though: he would always keep the Mafia a growing concern. He had made an oath to rep until his casket dropped, even if it was just by writing Southside Mafia on the cell wall so the next inmate to walk in the cell would see it. He wasn't letting the Mafia die.

He thought about all the things that led up to his present situation as he turned his back to the door and stuck his wrist out the tray flap so he could be handcuffed. He thought about all the people who wrote him off and turned their backs once he was sentenced. Surprisingly, even that brought a smile to his face. He learned that sometimes he had to let the gas run out to see who would get out and help him push.

Huncho and Cheeseboro walked to the elevator for the ride down to transport. "You think you're going home today?" Cheeseboro asked.

He shrugged. "Ain't no tellin'."

"What you going to court for?"

"I just got granted a new trial."

"That's what's up. Just make sure you do the right thing and stay out if you beat your case," Cheeseboro said sincerely.

Huncho smiled, thinking about the dream he just had. He knew if given the chance, he would never come back.

"Don't worry. I won't."

To Be Continued
Triggadale 2
Coming Soon

Submission Guideline

Submit the first three chapters of your completed manuscript to ldpsubmissions@gmail.com, subject line: Your book's title. The manuscript must be in a .doc file and sent as an attachment. Document should be in Times New Roman, double spaced and in size 12 font. Also, provide your synopsis and full contact information. If sending multiple submissions, they must each be in a separate email.

Have a story but no way to send it electronically? You can still submit to LDP/Ca$h Presents. Send in the first three chapters, written or typed, of your completed manuscript to:

LDP: Submissions Dept
Po Box 870494
Mesquite, Tx 75187

DO NOT send original manuscript. Must be a duplicate.

Provide your synopsis and a cover letter containing your full contact information.

Thanks for considering LDP and Ca$h Presents.

Triggadale
Coming Soon from Lock Down Publications/Ca$h Presents

BOW DOWN TO MY GANGSTA

By **Ca$h**

TORN BETWEEN TWO

By **Coffee**

BLOOD STAINS OF A SHOTTA **III**

By **Jamaica**

STEADY MOBBIN **III**

By **Marcellus Allen**

BLOOD OF A BOSS **V**

By **Askari**

LOYAL TO THE GAME **IV**

LIFE OF SIN

By **T.J. & Jelissa**

A DOPEBOY'S PRAYER **II**

By **Eddie "Wolf" Lee**

IF LOVING YOU IS WRONG... **III**

LOVE ME EVEN WHEN IT HURTS **II**

By **Jelissa**

TRUE SAVAGE **VI**

By **Chris Green**

BLAST FOR ME **III**

A BRONX TALE

By **Ghost**

ADDICTIED TO THE DRAMA **III**

By **Jamila Mathis**

LIPSTICK KILLAH **III**

CRIME OF PASSION **II**

Elijah R. Freeman

By **Mimi**

WHAT BAD BITCHES DO **III**

KILL ZONE **II**

By **Aryanna**

THE COST OF LOYALTY **II**

By **Kweli**

SHE FELL IN LOVE WITH A REAL ONE **II**

By **Tamara Butler**

LOVE SHOULDN'T HURT **III**

RENEGADE BOYS **II**

By **Meesha**

CORRUPTED BY A GANGSTA **III**

By **Destiny Skai**

A GANGSTER'S CODE **III**

By **J-Blunt**

KING OF NEW YORK III

By **T.J. Edwards**

CUM FOR ME **IV**

By **Ca$h & Company**

GORILLAS IN THE BAY

De'Kari

THE STREETS ARE CALLING

Duquie Wilson

KINGPIN KILLAZ II

Hood Rich

STEADY MOBBIN' **III**

Marcellus Allen

SINS OF A HUSTLER

ASAD

160

Triggadale
HER MAN, MINE'S TOO II
Nicole Goosby

GORILLAZ IN THE BAY II
DE'KARI

TRIGGADALE II
Elijah R. Freeman

Available Now

RESTRAINING ORDER I & II
By **CA$H & Coffee**

LOVE KNOWS NO BOUNDARIES I II & III
By **Coffee**

RAISED AS A GOON I, II, III & IV

BRED BY THE SLUMS I, II, III

BLAST FOR ME I & II

ROTTEN TO THE CORE I III
By **Ghost**

LAY IT DOWN I & II

LAST OF A DYING BREED

BLOOD STAINS OF A SHOTTA I & II
By **Jamaica**

LOYAL TO THE GAME

LOYAL TO THE GAME II

LOYAL TO THE GAME III
By **TJ & Jelissa**

BLOODY COMMAS I & II

SKI MASK CARTEL I II & III

KING OF NEW YORK I II

Elijah R. Freeman

By **T.J. Edwards**

IF LOVING HIM IS WRONG...I & II

LOVE ME EVEN WHEN IT HURTS

By **Jelissa**

WHEN THE STREETS CLAP BACK I & II III

By **Jibril Williams**

A DISTINGUISHED THUG STOLE MY HEART I II & III

LOVE SHOULDN'T HURT I II

RENEGADE BOYS

By **Meesha**

A GANGSTER'S CODE I & II

By **J-Blunt**

PUSH IT TO THE LIMIT

By **Bre' Hayes**

BLOOD OF A BOSS **I, II, III & IV**

By **Askari**

THE STREETS BLEED MURDER **I, II & III**

THE HEART OF A GANGSTA I II& III

By **Jerry Jackson**

CUM FOR ME

CUM FOR ME 2

CUM FOR ME 3

An **LDP Erotica Collaboration**

BRIDE OF A HUSTLA **I II & II**

THE FETTI GIRLS **I, II& III**

CORRUPTED BY A GANGSTA I & II

By **Destiny Skai**

WHEN A GOOD GIRL GOES BAD

By **Adrienne**

162

Triggadale

Elijah R. Freeman

THE ULTIMATE BETRAYAL

By **Phoenix**

BOSS'N UP **I , II & III**

By **Royal Nicole**

I LOVE YOU TO DEATH

By Destiny J

I RIDE FOR MY HITTA

I STILL RIDE FOR MY HITTA

By **Misty Holt**

LOVE & CHASIN' PAPER

By **Qay Crockett**

TO DIE IN VAIN

By **ASAD**

BROOKLYN HUSTLAZ

By **Boogsy Morina**

BROOKLYN ON LOCK I & II

By **Sonovia**

GANGSTA CITY

By **Teddy Duke**

A DRUG KING AND HIS DIAMOND I & II III

A DOPEMAN'S RICHES

HER MAN, MINE'S TOO

By Nicole Goosby

TRAPHOUSE KING **I II & III**

KINGPIN KILLAZ

By **Hood Rich**

LIPSTICK KILLAH **I, II**

CRIME OF PASSION

By **Mimi**

164

Triggadale

BOOKS BY LDP'S CEO, CA$H

TRUST IN NO MAN

TRUST IN NO MAN 2

TRUST IN NO MAN 3

BONDED BY BLOOD

SHORTY GOT A THUG

THUGS CRY

THUGS CRY 2

THUGS CRY 3

TRUST NO BITCH

TRUST NO BITCH 2

TRUST NO BITCH 3

TIL MY CASKET DROPS

RESTRAINING ORDER

RESTRAINING ORDER 2

IN LOVE WITH A CONVICT

Coming Soon

BONDED BY BLOOD 2

BOW DOWN TO MY GANGSTA

Triggadale